Kafka... for our time

Journeys of discovery

Michael Major

Harcourt Publishing UK

Copyright © Michael Major 2011

All rights reserved

No part of this book may be reproduced by any means, nor translated into a machine language, nor transmitted, without the written permission of the publisher.

The rights of Michael Major to be identified as the author of this work has been asserted in accordance with sections 77 and 78 of the Copyright, Design and Patents Act 1988.

Condition of Sale
This book is sold subject to the conditions that it shall not, by way of trade or otherwise, be lent, re-sold, hired out or otherwise circulated in any form of binding or cover other than that in which it is published and without a similar condition being imposed on the subsequent publisher.

Harcourt Publishing UK
harcourtpublishinguk@yahoo.com

Translated by Azadeh Medaglia, from the original short stories of Franz Kafka.

ISBN: 978-0-9567982-1-3

Dedicated with love and
appreciation to my dear friend

Azadeh

CONTENTS

INTRODUCTION I

BEFORE THE LAW 1

AN IMPERIAL MESSAGE..9

AN OLD MANUSCRIPT 13

A DREAM 23

THE SILENCE OF THE SIRENS 29

ON THE QUESTION OF LAWS 37

A FRATRICIDE...43

THE PASSENGER...49

THE NEW ADVOCATE 53

REFLECTIONS FOR GENTLEMEN-JOCKEYS 57

GIVE IT UP!..61

POSEIDON...65

ELEVEN SONS...71

UNMASKING OF A CONFIDENCE TRICKSTER 85

A CROSSBREED...91

THE CITY COAT OF ARMS..97

PROMETHEUS..105

FIRST SORROW 109

THE TRUTH ABOUT SANCHO PANZA 117

THE TEST 121

THE STREET WINDOW 127

JACKALS AND ARABS..129

REJECTION 139

METAMORPHOSIS...143

INTRODUCTION

The most powerful meaning and greatest beauty can be found in the simplest of things; where complication merely clouds the clarity of one's senses and judgement, simplicity allows openness and receptivity. I have grown to appreciate the value of keeping things simple, even when attempting to understand that which is considered to be complex: In this way, I can more easily make sense of what I learn, gaining a greater understanding... and potentially, the knowledge of how to use such things to enrich my life. This approach is the premise on which I have based my interpretations of some of Franz Kafka's work.

Kafka was born in Prague, Czechoslovakia, in 1883 to Jewish-German parentage; he acquired a Law degree and worked for an insurance company in his professional role, whilst devoting his personal time to writing works of fiction. He appeared to be a tormented soul, struggling with an inner turmoil and despair which seem all too evident in his literature. The severely strained relationship he had with his father, whom he considered to be emotionally abusive, along with him embracing his Jewish origins, must surely have contributed to his inner conflict, especially as the social climate in Czechoslovakia at that time was inimical to the Jewish culture. He published very little of his work during his lifetime – preferring to write for personal enjoyment rather than for a need to share – and after a two year battle with tuberculosis he died in 1924 at the age of forty. Kafka left instructions with his close friend Max Brod to destroy all of his unpublished works after his death; however Brod chose to ignore this request, as he considered Kafka's work far too important; he thus brought much of this unpublished work into the public domain, which resulted in Kafka becoming greatly revered posthumously. Kafka's work is noted for its apparent absurdity, for it possesses – for those like myself who have no deep understanding of his style – no clear point or purpose: And it is for this reason that the term "Kafkaesque" has come into fashion, for many situations that appear absurd can be described by this expression.

For most of my life I had no knowledge of Franz Kafka, let alone an appreciation of his work or the impact it has had on literature. I was introduced to Kafka's work purely by chance, when a dear friend outlined 'Before The Law' to me: Its puzzling content appeared intriguing, compelling me to try and make sense of it. The fact that 'Before The Law' was one of Kafka's most famous parables was of no consequence to me, but this one – like all the subsequent stories I have interpreted – was so unlike the literature I was used to reading, that it became a tantalising challenge to unravel the mystery within. The distinguishing feature of Franz Kafka's work appears to be its absurdity, the lack of a defined point which one can readily identify. Instead, his work forces you to read it again, and then again, inspiring questions that demand answers: Why has he written this story this way? Why did he choose this subject matter? Is he trying to provide a lesson or is it merely an insightful observation? Is Kafka trying to share his own personal feelings with the reader in hope of understanding and empathy, or is his work simply a kind of private therapy for him to purge himself of his own personal turmoil? How can I gain a meaningful insight from his work that will be purposeful to my life? Ironically, it is this absurdity that creates the appeal, inviting the readers to seek their own conclusion: This offers them the opportunity to contemplate Kafka's literature by the standards of their own intellect and imagination, encouraging them to consider its relevance not only to the man himself, but also to their personal journey of discovery.

I, by no stretch of the imagination, consider this book to provide any definitive answers! I do not propose to offer the reader a lesson, nor any form of instruction, for I do not believe I have any conclusive solutions to the puzzles that exist within Kafka's work.

I do however prefer to think of this book as an invitation to others... to offer their own contribution; and in so doing, I hope to create an opportunity for them to share their thoughts on Kafka as I have shared mine. It is reasonable to assume that Kafka's work was a reflection of himself, a written expression of his journey, as he lived out his life through the characters he wrote about and the predicaments he placed them in. Through the medium of his work, Kafka presents himself to us, either consciously or subconsciously... as a reflection of his soul appears to be imprinted on every story. Therefore, I hope to have gained through my interpretations a greater understanding of the man himself, of his work, of the world in which he lived, and through this, of the world in which I live, my own life, and ultimately... myself!

Michael Major

BEFORE THE LAW

Before the Law stands a gatekeeper. A man from the countryside approaches the gatekeeper and begs for entry into the Law; the gatekeeper says he could not grant him admission at the moment. The man considers this, then enquires whether he would be permitted entry at a later time. 'It is possible,' says the gatekeeper, 'but not now'. Since the gate to the Law remains open as usual and the gatekeeper has stepped to one side, the man bends forward to peer inside. Detecting this, the gatekeeper says laughing: 'If it so entices you, then just try to enter, despite my refusal. Beware however: I am powerful, and I am only the nethermost gatekeeper. There are other gatekeepers, in each hall, one more powerful than the next. Even I could not endure the sight of the third one!' The man from the countryside had not anticipated such troubles; he believes the Law should indeed be accessible to everyone, and at all times. However, as he watches the gatekeeper clad in his fur coat more closely, with his large pointed nose, the long, sparse, black, tartaric beard, he decides holding off until he could get permission to accede. The gatekeeper gives him a stool and lets him take a seat to one side of the gate. There he sits for days... leading to years. He attempts many times to gain entry, and wearies the gatekeeper by his entreaties. Occasionally the doorkeeper questions him in order to sound him out, quizzing him about his homeland and many other things; these enquiries are however indifferent and apathetic, like those asked by great lords, and at the end he always tells him, that he cannot let him enter yet. The man had arrived fully equipped for his journey, but foregoes all he possesses and anything that may be of value, in order to entice the gatekeeper. The latter accepts all he is offered, but adds at the same time: 'I only accept so that you do not think you have neglected something.' Over the years, the man almost uninterruptedly observes the gatekeeper. He forgets the other

1

gatekeepers, for this first one appears to him as the sole impediment to his entry into the Law. He curses his misfortune, in the first years heedless and loudly but later, as he gets older ...he only mumbles to himself. He becomes childish, and since during years of observing the gatekeeper he has come to know even the fleas in his fur collar, he pleads with the insects to intervene on his behalf and bring the gatekeeper round. In the end his eyesight fails and he wonders whether the world around is a darker place or his eyes are deluding him. Yet he discerns a sparkle in the dark, shining inextinguishably through the doors of the Law. Now he does not have long to live. At the threshold of death, all he has ever experienced gathers into a single question in his mind, a question he had not put to the gatekeeper until now. He beckons him over as he cannot set his stiffened body upright anymore. The gatekeeper has to stoop quite low for their difference in height has altered much, and to the man's great disadvantage. 'What is it that you still wish to know?' asks the gatekeeper. 'You are insatiable'. 'Indeed everyone aspires to explore the Law,' says the man, 'why is it then that in all these years, no one else called for admittance?' The gatekeeper recognises that the man has indeed reached the end of his days, and in order to catch his now failing hearing, roars in his ear: 'No one else could have obtained admittance here, for this gateway was intended solely for you. I will now finally close it'.

INTERPRETATION

Kafka now extends an invitation to his readers to take their place ...*Before The Law*: Though not in the defence of one's innocence, instead... to preside in judgement over one's inaction! One of the author's more notable works, *Before The Law* may ingeniously illustrate how giving way to Fear can dramatically alter the course of our lives, with devastating consequences!

Fear is one of the most powerful and all-consuming emotions, possessing an unquenchable appetite for control, as it feeds on our worries and doubts: Ironically, this in-built mechanism of protection – our instinctive cautiousness – is all too frequently assigned to many of our day-to-day affairs, making our lives miserable. If the three main subjects in Kafka's story are metaphors for Ourselves, something of great interest to us, and the fear related to that interest…then a fascinating meaning unfolds: The man from the countryside is a representation of Ourselves, striving to explore a new possibility; the Law is symbolic of something of great interest, new and significant …drawing us in; the gatekeeper is an illustration of our fear, the menacing beast that stands at the threshold of a new experience, halting progress.

'Before the law stands a gatekeeper' illustrates that before our ambitions, desires, interests, hopes and longings …stands our Fear! The man from the countryside arrives before the gatekeeper, seeking permission to enter the Law, but is refused entry at this time; though the gatekeeper informs the man that he may be granted admission at an unspecified future time, he gives no reason for his refusal. Here we see how Fear, acting out of instinct, stands at the threshold of each new possibility, intervening to shield us from potential harm, but instead, acts like a menacing bully trying to frighten and control us; going so far as to tease us with the possibility of having what we want at some future time, only to once again stand in the way when that time arrives!

Since the gate to the Law stands open, and the man's curiosity is strong, he endeavours to see inside the Law; the gatekeeper sees this and tells the man he is welcome to ignore his refusal… but what he will face once inside will be far worse. The man heeds this warning, surprised by the predicament he now faces, and after studying the gatekeeper's appearance, believes it is best to take his word. Despite our fear standing in the way, our curiosity does not diminish, nor does it prevent us from wanting to pry, if only a

3

little. However, when fear recognises that we are not deterred by its initial warning, it will try to convince us that to ignore it and proceed… will lead to even greater dangers ahead; fear itself is nothing more than an illusion created within our mind, a result of our overactive imagination. The man sees the gatekeeper, as we may see our fear, as something far stronger and more dangerous than it really is… so we relent and try to appease it. The gatekeeper offers the man a seat beside the doorway to the Law, and regularly questions his unsuspecting guest, though these enquiries are somewhat condescending, and without specific interest or concern for the answers. This suggests that Fear now amuses itself at our expense, allowing us to sit so close to our desires, questioning us with the dispassionate disinterest of a great lord …for now it has become our master, and all the while reminding us that we may not proceed.

The man sacrifices everything he possesses to the gatekeeper, believing he can use this as leverage to win his admittance into the Law; the gatekeeper takes all he is offered without reluctance or gratitude, and always claims he is doing this with the man's best interests in mind. How easily we would sacrifice all we own, in the vain hope that our fear will relent, only to find that this fear will take it all, stripping us bare of everything valuable, including our dignity, and always with the pretence that this is done for our benefit! The many years of patiently sitting by the Law has resulted in the man's attention becoming transfixed on the gatekeeper, causing him to completely forget about the other gatekeepers who allegedly exist; the close scrutiny of the gatekeeper has made him aware of even the fleas on this guardian's collar, with whom he often pleads to intervene so as to change their host's mind. Whilst seated at his station, the man regularly denounces his foul fortune, with great vigour in his earlier years, but more soberly when he grows older. One can so easily become transfixed on fear, consumed by only this fear, as all else is forgotten. The smallest features of our fear take great significance, as we define even the tiniest detail around it; if only the man from the countryside had brushed this gatekeeper aside and entered the Law... he would not hold such power over the man; similarly, if only we brush our fear aside... it would not hold such power over us. If we allow our progress to be halted by fear, all that will remain for us will be to curse our misfortune.

The man's eyesight has become tainted, for the many years of obediently waiting have taken their toll; despite this, he still believes he sees the light from the doors to the Law shining evermore brightly, though he is uncertain whether this is his imagination or the eternal brilliance radiating from this great attraction. The man, now close to his end, has only one question to ask; he thus summons over the gatekeeper who throws scorn on his insatiable persistence; unlike the gatekeeper, the man has deteriorated much over the years... forcing the gatekeeper to bend down to meet his level. Though the years may take their toll on our body, draining our physical strength and dulling our senses, the brilliance that radiates from our desires continues to hold its allure: Even if we surrender to fear, our ambitions and dreams continue to shine in our hearts 'inextinguishably'.

The man poses his question, aware that everybody aspires to reach the Law... but no one but himself has ever asked for entry to this doorway. The gatekeeper now recognises that the man is no longer capable of entering the Law, so he reveals the devastating truth, that this doorway, leading to the Law, was exclusively for the use of the man from the countryside, and now it will be closed and he will go. This startling revelation illustrates that fear stands at the entry to one person's opportunity; an opportunity that exists uniquely for the exploration and progress of only that person; and when that person's life comes to an end, so does that opportunity ...along with its associated fear! If only the man had the courage to walk past the gatekeeper, to enter the doorway to the Law, and explore that... which attracted him so strongly in the first place, how different his life would have been. Instead, he sought permission from the gatekeeper, he believed what this guardian told him, he squandered his life remaining outside that which he longed to explore, he sacrificed all he possessed without success, he became preoccupied with this gatekeeper and his pet fleas, and allowed his life to pass idly by...only to see the gatekeeper take all he had and close the doors to the Law in his face!

Do we need permission from our fear to explore what we desire, will we allow fear to dictate how we proceed, shall we sacrifice all ...only to have fear take everything and leave us without even our dignity, are we prepared to squander our opportunities ...only to see life passing by? Will we allow fear to roar its final insult into our ear... as we see the gateway to our opportunity close forever and watch our illusory fear disappear? Well ...will you?

BEFORE THE LAW

My curiosity had brought me ...to the gates of The Law
But all progress was halted... I could venture no more

A Gatekeeper there stood... who obstructed my path
With his menacing demeanour ...and a soul filled with wrath

Warning not to continue... on my journey ahead
For more frightening will face me: The thought filled me with
dread

Though my hunger for knowledge... of what lay inside
Simply would not relent ...it just would not subside

But he held firm with his caution... of the immanent danger
So now who do I trust ...myself or this stranger?

Held back with uncertainty, burdened with apprehension
Unsure of my fate... I'm held here in suspension

So I patiently waited, hoping he would relent
But time just marched on, with opportunities spent

As my life drifted on, and the years passed me by
All that remained... was just waiting to die

The end brought me courage... to enquire of this gate
Though I was informed, it was just for my fate

And thus when I am gone, it will be closed up and locked
I've no time to be sorry, nor time to be shocked

I think of all those ambitions, of those things I've desired
For the unique opportunities... that left me inspired

Although I look back and wish for... this chance once again
It is time to accept... this is where I'll remain

But the long-term companion I chose ...it was fear
Controlling my choices... it drove me to despair

So now at the end... I am filled with regret
The price that I've paid ...is a terrible debt

And what of the lesson ...I chose to endure?
It was my time spent in judgement... Before The Law!

AN IMPERIAL MESSAGE

Legend has it that the Emperor has sent you a message: to you...
his pathetic solitary subject, fleeing the imperial sunlight into the
remotest shadows; yes ...precisely to you, has the Emperor sent a
message from his deathbed. He had the messenger kneel by the
bed, and he then whispered the message in his ear; it was of such
great concern to him, that he had him whisper it back to him. By a
nod of the head, he affirmed the accuracy of the statement. Before
the eyes of the onlookers of his final hours – all the impeding
walls have been knocked down and on the wide and high flight of
stairs, stand in a circle, the great and the good of the land – before
all these, he has dispatched the message. The messenger starts his
journey at once. A strong and indefatigable man; thrusting out first
one arm, then the other, he negotiates his way through the crowd;
should he encounter resistance, he shows the symbol of the sun on
his chest; he goes forth nimbly as no one could. However, the
gatherings are immense and the dwellings countless. Had it been
an open field, how fast would he fly and you would indeed hear
the glorious knock of his fists on your door ...before long. Instead,
he trudges on needlessly; he worms his way through the chambers
of the innermost palace; he would never surmount this hurdle; had
he even been capable of doing so, he would gain nothing; he
would have to fight his way down the stairs; and had he been able
to do so, nothing would be gained; he would still have to cross the
courts; and afterwards the second outer palace; and once again
flights of stairs and courtyards; and again a palace; and so on ...for
a thousand years; and should he at last fall out of the outermost
gate – but never, can that happen – the imperial capital would lie
before him, at the centre of the world, heaped high full of its dregs.
No one could get through here, even with a message from the
dead. You however... sit at your window and dream of it, when
evening falls.

INTERPRETATION

Shall we foster the hope, or even dare to dream, that our humble life, insignificant as it may be in the grand scheme of world affairs, so far removed from the ones who preside over us in reverence and authority, will one day be worthy of ...*An Imperial Message*? This significant message, bringing hope to a distant soul, is the connection that one longs for. From deep within one's essence, stirs a yearning for recognition, a wish for acknowledgement, from those one holds aloft in high esteem. Though we may be considered as nothing more than a subject of a Monarch or a number at a ballot box, it is through our loyal devotion that these figureheads remain in reverent authority. Our struggle may often be great, with many years of arduous toil, and though we may never be the first thought on these peoples' mind, or even a fleeting consideration to them, we hope that we will at the very least ...be the last!

This wish for an incredible message, uniquely for you, uttered from the lips of the noblest in the land, is surely the greatest desire for any devout subject. Though leagues of people stand between you and this great man, with so many bearing greater significance, well beyond your humble dominion, to feel worthy enough to take precedence over all others, keeps your spirit of belief alive. Never before have you received the acknowledgement of such a mighty person, nor has he ever sought you out with such purpose, but now, at this most poignant moment...you are his worthiest subject. So vital is his message, that he seeks reassurance from the messenger that it has been taken in: Choosing to whisper, for it is the messenger alone who should hear his voice. Only when this all-powerful ruler is satisfied is his consent given, for now it is time to deliver the precious gift: The witnesses to this momentous event are the most senior and significant; despite their prominence, the Emperor's words are meant only for the least likely of all.

It is only the mightiest of messengers who is chosen for the task, armed with single-minded determination to deliver the precious message. However, the obstacles before him are many and the paths ahead insurmountable, so his persistence, though admirable …is futile. The messenger strives to pass through the palace, the courtyards, and the crowds, in hope of reaching the open fields where he will soar away on his journey; but his path will never be clear, for one obstacle after another present themselves, trapping him in an endless maze: Should this message-bearer finally overcome the confines of the palace, not that he will, but should he, an even more daunting prospect lies ahead… that of a city which holds greater obstacles to breach. Though the great messenger is determined, the odds are stacked against him, for Fate has placed what must be an unconquerable gauntlet to run: There is no one who could overcome these obstacles, no one who could deliver any message, regardless of who bestowed it …or its meaning! Despite the frustration and despair, you sit by your window and wishfully gaze out, in hope that one day destiny will enable a mighty messenger to find his way to your door… so he can finally deliver *An Imperial Message*.

So what of this message today, relating to our modern times… where could it be, when will it arrive …and who is the mighty messenger who will bring it? Perhaps this great message is already here …illustrated in Kafka's work, revealing the nature of our society…and of each of us. Could parallels be drawn from this message and the failures in our political system, where core ideas for improving society become distorted and displaced when entangled in the bureaucratic system, never finding their way through the unnecessary red-tape… and becoming shamefully lost in translation? Could we contemplate this message as an appeal from the soul, trying to find a way through the maze of emotions and obstacles thrown up by the subconscious? Or maybe… *An Imperial Message* reflects Kafka's writing and its connection to his readers; a valuable message bestowed by this Emperor of literature, delivered by the indefatigable style of his writing, intended for those most distantly placed from mainstream ideology, its meaning never arriving …as it is constantly confronted by the barriers of conventionalism!

AN OLD MANUSCRIPT

It appears much has been neglected in the defence of our homeland. Until now, we have not given it a great deal of careful thought, and have only pursued our own daily work. Recent events however, have begun to make us uneasy.

I have a cobbler's repair shop in the square opposite the Emperor's palace. At dawn, scarcely have I opened my doors, that I see the entrance of all incoming streets to the square occupied by armed soldiers. They are however not our soldiers, but nomads from the North. In a manner which is beyond my grasp, they have managed to infiltrate our town's capital, which is in fact so far removed from the frontiers. Anyhow, they are here now; it seems as if every morning there are more of them.

True to their nature, they encamp outdoors, for they loathe dwelling houses. They busy themselves by sharpening their swords, tapering their arrows and working out with their horses. They have literally made a stable out of this quiet town square which had always been so scrupulously maintained. Sometimes we do try to walk forth from our shops and at least remove the worst of the effluent, but this is happening ever more seldom, for the effort is futile, moreover it puts us in danger of being trampled by the wild horses or being lashed and wounded.

One cannot speak with the nomads. They do not understand our language, and they do not have any of their own. They communicate amongst themselves in a language similar to that of jackdaws. One hears constantly the screech of the jackdaws. Our lifestyle, our institutions, are as incomprehensible to them as indifferent. As a result, they refuse to communicate even with sign language. You could wrench your jaw and contort your hands out of their joints, for they do not understand you and will never understand you. Often they grimace; then the whites of their eyes turn upwards and froth spills out of their mouths; by that, they do not mean to frighten nor imply anything; they merely do it because it is their nature. Whatever they want, they take. It cannot be said they use violence. When they snatch something one simply stands to one side and cedes everything.

They have also often taken many fine pieces from my stock. However, I cannot complain about that, when for instance I see what has befallen the butcher across the way. As soon as he brings in his commodities, all are snatched and devoured by the nomads. Even their horses eat flesh; often a rider lies beside his horse and they both feed from the same piece of meat, one at each end. The butcher is fearful and does not dare stop the meat delivery. We understand that, we collect money and we all support him. If the Nomads get no meat, who knows what they might think of doing; indeed who knows what they might think of doing anyway, even when they get meat daily!

A while ago, the butcher thought he could at least spare himself the effort of slaughtering, and brought along a live ox in the morning. He should never repeat that in future. I lay on the floor right in the back of my workshop and stacked all my clothes, blankets and cushions on myself, just so as not to hear the bellows of the ox, for the Nomads sprang forth from all sides to tear away at its living flesh with their teeth. It had been quite a long time, before I dared going out; like drinkers at a wine barrel, they lay exhausted all around the carcass of the ox.

Just then I thought I had seen the Emperor at a window of his palace; he usually never comes to these outer rooms and always lives in the innermost garden; but this time he stood, or at least it so appeared to me, at one of the windows and looked on with lowered head, at the hustle and bustle before his castle.

'What is going to happen?' we all ask ourselves. 'How long will we be able to bear this burden and agony?' The Emperor's palace has attracted the Nomads, but he does not know how to disperse them again. The gate remains shut, the guard who was always

14

solemnly marching in and out, now keeps himself behind barred windows. The salvation of our homeland has been entrusted to us artisans and tradesmen; but we are not adept for this task nor have we after all ever been equipped for it. This is a misunderstanding, and it will lead us to our perdition.

INTERPRETATION

An Old Manuscript aptly reflects the conditions that affect many peace-loving people throughout the world, as their harmonious existence is shattered by the thoughtless and disruptive actions of others migrating into their habitat. Kafka's tale of decline and hopelessness holds parallels with three significant issues affecting societies throughout the ages. The first illustrates how the contrasting cultural and social make-up of different groups can clash, creating disharmony and conflict when they are forced to share the same space. The second relates to the importance of maintaining one's traditions and core values. The last refers to the need for those in positions of authority to serve and protect their subjects honourably, within their governing duties.

The world is populated with a richly diverse blend of ethnicities, all possessing unique cultural differences and social intricacies. The traditions and religious beliefs of each tribe have developed through the natural course of evolution, as a result of the environmental and historical interaction with the world around them. Certain cultures may appear to be more advanced, others more primitive, some feel gentle and tolerant whilst others seem hostile and uncompromising, but each one's evolution has been significant for its survival. Problems can arise, and so often do, when these diverse cultures try to co-exist within close proximity, without being respectful or considerate to one another.

It is all too easy for a particular group to become complacent about maintaining its traditional social system. This appears to be especially prevalent in tolerant cultures, where there is little or no threat to their way of life. As complacency increases, so does the risk to the established system, when challenged by a less compromising external cultural force. A group that does not uphold the necessary defence of its system, and is tolerant of an uncompromising culture, may risk sacrificing its own way of life altogether.

Those who govern us have a dual obligation to honour: To lead us responsibly in times of peace, as well as defend us honourably in times of trouble. It is all too easy for these authoritative figures to be courted by the trappings of power and forget their responsibilities; this applies to all leaders, whether elected or not. By entrusting our way of life to a governing authority, we leave ourselves powerless... blindly unaware that we have become servants to those who should be serving us. Ironically, in times of crisis it all too often appears that the loyal subjects are left to struggle for survival, whilst the so-called leaders fight to preserve their position and privilege.

The peaceful townsfolk had lived in harmony until they were gradually over-run by the war ravaged soldiers. As each day passes...more soldiers arrive, until the sheer number of these invading marauders overwhelm the town; now the townsfolk completely lose the state of harmonious normality they once took for granted. Despite their demeanour, these soldiers do not mean to be enemies of the town, and are only looking for shelter away from the front line of battle; they none-the-less turn this peaceful place into a training ground for war, as they practice and prepare for further conflict. The fact that the town is an inappropriate place to do this is irrelevant, as the soldiers are unaware they are doing anything wrong. However, the townsfolk are peaceful civilians, and standing up to their uninvited guests seems far too frightening and potentially dangerous. Though they try to continue as normal, they are forced to adapt to a new and more hostile environment. This aptly illustrates how one's harmonious way of life can change quickly and dramatically... if one does not act to protect and preserve it. To be too accommodating or complacent carries the risk of becoming overwhelmed by an external force too powerful to control or remove.

The townsfolk find communicating with the soldiers impossible, for they have no wish to communicate either verbally or through gesturing: Despite this, the cobbler recognises that the responses from the soldiers – though strange and incomprehensible – are not meant to be threatening. This exemplifies how the language barrier can create difficulties forging lines of communication with others from a different origin, especially if they have no desire to do so in the first place. This predicament can be especially frustrating and wholly unpleasant if these outsiders undertake the same actions as the soldiers, and do as they wish without care or concern for the consequences: If they remain unwilling to communicate with their new – even if somewhat reluctant – hosts, they will always appear to be hostile and unacceptable

The townspeople are now forced to retreat, to run and hide from a most distressing scene... that of the Ox being torn apart by the soldiers who devour the unfortunate beast alive: The unconscionable behaviour of these nomads, coupled with the gruesome sight and sounds of the Ox's distress, leave the cobbler in complete despair as to the fate of the town. Kafka may have used this incident to symbolise the brutality and disregard an external force can demonstrate towards the very sustenance of the system it invades; where the townsfolk would be compassionate towards the animal, the soldiers show no concern for its pain and suffering... tearing the beast apart despite its obvious distress.

At the aftermath of the incident with the Ox, the cobbler emerges from his shop and looks up at the Imperial palace... where he

17

believes he sees the Emperor looking out from his high-walled, well guarded haven at the mayhem of the town he governs. The cobbler remarks that he does not see the palace gates opening anymore, he does not see the Emperor take action to drive these nomads away, and it is up to him and his fellow townspeople to endure this ghastly and uncertain state of affairs for the unforeseeable future. This highlights the dishonourable and self-serving nature of those who call themselves leaders, who command respect and demand allegiance from their subjects …but fail to defend and protect when duty calls. Does this Emperor open his palace gates to let his subjects in for protection? Does he send soldiers out to fend off the invaders and bring normality back to his town? Does he demonstrate the bravery and honour required to make him a worthy leader? Or is he instead a coward who hides behind his high walls, behind the protection of the soldiers he commands, offering no defence, allowing his subjects to fend for themselves, with his most daring act being one of venturing to a window high-up in his palace to assess the carnage in the town? How similar this scenario is to circumstances we live under today, where leaders – either elected or hereditary – enjoy the privilege and power of office when times are good… but flee from their responsibilities and duties when the time for action arrives!

Is it possible that *An Old Manuscript* is Kafka's first-hand experience of the decline in society, his recognition of the strain of cultural integration, coupled with the abandonment of important core values and failures in good governance? How very purposeful it may have been for Kafka to choose a Cobbler as the story's protagonist, for this tradesman's profession is literally to keep people's feet firmly on the ground, and who better to share the experience of the common man than someone who helps him maintain his connection to common ground!? This thought-provoking story may offer a timely reminder, as well as an indirect warning… for the need to fiercely defend and protect those things that shape and define who we are, what we have, where we live …and what our ancestors have fought so determinedly to achieve. Though others may choose to migrate into our space, either through curiosity or necessity, the established system that has been built by our forefathers and maintained by ourselves …should not be disregarded or inadvertently lost through weakness or complacency. The warning continues to remind us that if we are willing to show understanding, compromise and respect to strangers, then these must demonstrate the same deference for the established traditions. There is yet another moral to this story, no less important: That power and control should always remain in the hands of the people…and not be surrendered to only a handful of individuals who claim leadership. These principles are fundamental for our future welfare and happiness …and ultimately, even our very survival may depend on it!

AN OLD MANUSCRIPT

They came from afar… invading our space
Appearing in droves… this nomadic race

Destroying the harmony… that once soothed our town
Besieged by these strangers …in their midst we will drown

Conducting their business… with no thought for us
We've no power to stop them… we do not dare fuss

They take what they want… fulfilling their needs
As our haemorrhaging town, continually bleeds

So wild and so savage… with no graces or vanity
We are losing what's ours, barely left is our sanity

Where do we turn now, who will hear our calls?
The leader we know …hides behind his high walls

Overlooking the carnage, from his distant position
Protecting his privilege, is his only mission

To stand-up for what's right, in this desperate hour
We are in need of our saviour… not to hide in his tower

Thus we are left here to stand, and endure this wild pack
With no time for inaction, or a chance to turn back

Shall the fate of the Ox… be the same for us All?
Do we now face destruction …are we destined to fall?

Suffering the consequence... of complacencies' lesson
Is a costly mistake ...and a painful confession

Our forefathers forged... our customs from history
So we wouldn't be left... in confusion and mystery

But how much did we treasure ...this priceless gift?
Was it held close to our hearts... or set off adrift?

Shall we resign our existence ...to history's Crypt?
Or uphold the wisdom... of An Old Manuscript!

A DREAM

He had barely taken a couple of steps when he already found himself at the cemetery. The paths there were artificially made and impractically winding, but he floated over them as if on flowing water, with an unshakable elegant poise. From a distance he caught sight of a freshly dug grave-mound, next to which he decided to pause. The mound was wielding a strange fascination, he could barely wait to reach it. Occasionally he would lose sight of the mound, for it was concealed behind flags that flapped forcefully, entwining one-another. One could not see the flag-bearers, but it seemed that there reigned a great celebration.

As he gazed into the distance, he suddenly saw the same grave-mound right beside him on the path, and then immediately behind him. He sprang hastily onto the grass. The earth was giving way under his shifting foot and he tottered and fell on his knees just in front of the mound. Two men, standing behind the grave, were holding between them a stone in the air. Just as K. arrived, they thrust it onto the earth and it stood there as if cemented. A third man, whom K. recognised as an artist, instantly stepped out from behind a bush. He was clad in a pair of trousers and a badly buttoned shirt. He wore a velvet cap on his head and in his hand held a simple pencil with which he was already drawing shapes in the air.

Pencil in hand, he now attended to the gravestone; the stone was way too high; he did not have to bend at all although he had to lean forward, for the mound on which he did not want to tread, separated him from the stone. He stood on tiptoe and with his left hand poised himself on the surface of the stone. With artful ingenious skill, he succeeded in inscribing golden letters with the same ordinary pencil. He wrote: 'Here lies... '. Each letter appeared limpid and beautiful, deeply incised, in the purest gold. Having composed the two words, the artist then turned around to look at K. who was eagerly observing the inscription and did not care at all about the man: His gaze was instead fixed on the stone. The artist intended to continue his inscription, but he could not, there was a hindrance; he let the pencil drop and looked back at K. once more. This time K. took notice of the artist as well, recognising his deep embarrassment; he just could not fathom the reason. All his prior vivacity had now vanished.

This left K. feeling abashed as well; they exchanged helpless glances; there had arisen a grotesque misunderstanding which neither could resolve. An untimely little chapel bell began to ring, but the artist gestured with his hand and it stopped. A little while later it started again; this time softly and without urgency. It soon broke off, as if this little bell wanted to verify its own sound. K. was inconsolable on account of the artist's predicament. He began to cry and sobbed for a long time into his cupped hands. The artist waited until K. had calmed down and then, for lack of an alternative, decided to continue with his inscription. The first little stroke he composed, felt like a relief for K.; but this was obviously brought about by the artist with tremendous reluctance; above all, the inscription was not so beautiful anymore, the gold was less pronounced; the stroke seemed pale and uncertain, it just turned into a large letter. It was a J, but it was hardly completed when the artist stamped his foot so furiously on the grave-mound that the earth around flew into the air. At last K. understood him; there was no time for apologizing; he started digging into the earth…which did not put up any resistance at all; all seemed to be prepared; a thin crust of earth had been constructed, as if to keep up appearances; just beneath it, there opened a gaping hole with sloping walls, into which sank K., just as a gentle current stroked him on the back. As he was being swallowed into impenetrable depths, still straining to hold his neck high, his name raced across the stone, high up, in mighty bursts.

INTERPRETATION

Kafka appears to delve into the unfathomable workings of the subconscious mind, to illustrate how it plays out its own reality through the surrealism of a dream. It is only in a slumberous state that our dreams come to life, allowing that which is stored away deep within …to surface; this theatre show of the mind can so often leave us bewildered in our conscious state, as we awaken only to question the point and purpose of the dream. Though dreams may appear to be nothing more than a drama played out during sleep, these enigmatic dramatisations of the restless subconscious may be a key that opens the door to a valuable message of guidance from deep within.

The main character of this short story is Josef K., who is also the protagonist in one of Kafka's most famous works …*The Trial*. In that, Josef K. awakens one morning to find himself arrested and tried for an unspecified crime, the reasons for which are never made clear. Whether there is a connection between these two stories and the central character's predicament is purely a matter for the reader to determine, but whatever the case may be, it is clear Kafka designated two harrowing experiences for Josef K. to endure. Is it conceivable that both *The Trial* and *A Dream*, are reflections of Kafka's subconscious feelings… inadvertently expressed through his conscious writing style: Where *The Trial* represents his deepest thoughts about Guilt, *A Dream* broaches the subject of Mortality?!

Josef K. sets off for his walk on this beautiful day, quite unaware of the journey ahead or the destiny that awaits him, and shortly after, inadvertently arrives at a cemetery. This appears to illustrate how the subconscious takes us on what initially seems to be a purely innocent journey, not wishing to frighten or overwhelm us with the fear of what lies ahead, merely allowing us to get underway before unexpectedly transporting us where it wants us to be. Is it possible that Kafka's subconscious chose the destination for him to be a cemetery, needing to familiarise its host with his final resting place? This journey so necessary, as terminal illness took hold of him so prematurely. K. thought the paths to be unnatural and complicated, but found no difficulty negotiating them, for he wafted along with confident ease. Does this illustrate Kafka's subconscious confidence, allowing him to glide along, negotiating the maze of paths that would normally confuse his conscious mind, using his intuition to guide him through life's confusions? Josef K.'s attention was strangely drawn to the newly excavated grave-mound, implying that Kafka's subconscious may have been trying to introduce him to his newly unveiled feelings about mortality. The grave exerted a peculiar fascination over K., who desperately wished to arrive before it, occasionally losing sight of it. Could Kafka's curiosity compel him to explore the intriguing attraction at the heart of his dream – and as quickly as possible – though occasionally losing sight of the goal as obstructions blocked his view…with his ego disrupting the flow of this dream?

K. found himself suddenly next to the grave-mound, then just as quickly it was behind him. This may signify that Kafka's instinctive purpose was stronger than his egotistical distractions, allowing his thoughts to wander but ultimately return to the original objective, as he seized the moment before it was lost. The path was collapsing beneath K.'s feet, forcing him to leap reluctantly onto the grass, causing him to stumble and fall onto his knees in front of the grave. Kafka may have believed his path in life to be uncertain at times, often giving way beneath his feet, forcing him to leap off unexpectedly. He may have felt the pace and manner of progress in life was not always of his making… and that the flowing current of destiny carried him along this path, occasionally causing him to stumble and fall.

26

K.'s arrival at the grave resulted in the two men holding the gravestone, thrusting it into position, soon followed by the appearance of an artist whom K. recognised straight-away; this artist, dressed indistinctly and holding just an ordinary pencil, was drawing symbols in the air as he approached. Could this artist signify Kafka's fate? With no lavish clothes nor impressive tools at its disposal, just a simple figure appearing unexpectedly to undertake a significant task; for it is not how Fate appears that matters, but ultimately ...the writing it sets in stone! The stone was tall and the grave mound soft, causing the artist to rise on tiptoe as he sank into the soft earth; he had to bend forward, but was not forced to stoop down to write his inscription. Here Fate endeavours to leave its imprint ...regardless of the ground it stands on!

The artist produced 'limpid and beautiful' golden letters from his simple pencil, mesmerising K. who stood watching intently. After inscribing two words he turned to look at K. who continued to stare at the letters and ignored him... he tried to carry on but could not, out of embarrassment. The artist lost his 'vivacity', and turned once more to face K., who now recognised he too was embarrassed. Is it possible that deep down Kafka believed Fate itself would have felt embarrassed for the unfortunate role it played in his life, as this intervention was some kind of 'grotesque misunderstanding'? The untimely little chapel bell ringing out that caused the artist to signal with his hand to stop it, could represent the metaphorical dawning of the end, or more relevantly for Kafka, the dawning of his end... ringing out to instruct Fate to continue with its mission despite its reluctance. The bell rang again, this time more softly, presenting a less audible distraction but none the less a distant and constant reminder to Fate that its work must be done. Despite K.'s distress, the artist continued with his work, his efforts less admirable this time, becoming enraged after completing only one letter. K. now understood the message that the artist was conveying...and accepted his fate. Was Kafka implying his initial curiosity had now been replaced by acceptance, as he saw Fate inscribing his destiny onto the headstone, his subconscious reassuring him that with each step he took ...Fate added the finishing touches to complete the picture? The grave itself appeared to be ready for its occupant, offering little resistance to K., allowing him to descend into 'impenetrable depths', with his name completed rapidly on the stone. Kafka may concede that once we have accepted our fate, we smoothly move forward and fulfil destiny's prophecy. This entire process may have been a sweet relief for Kafka, the reassuring journey he needed to take in his mind: Encouraging him to accept that his life – like some of his literature – would end unexpectedly!

Dreams are the animated emotional energies held within the vaults of the mind, acting as a vital release for one's pent-up frustrations, as well as potentially valuable tool offering insightful guidance. The emotional release that cannot be satisfied in a conscious state, will strive to find its way out during sleep. The important lessons within these dreams are rich with symbolic messages from deep within, alerting our conscious self that life is impacting on us regularly at a much deeper level. Should a dream be considered only as a figment of the imagination... or a reflection of reality from the deepest realms of one's essence?

THE SILENCE OF THE SIRENS

Proof that even simple, indeed childish measures could conduce to redemption!

To protect himself from the Sirens, Odysseus filled his ears with wax – and had himself secured to his ship's mast. All along, seafarers could of course have done the same, except for those whom the Sirens had already allured, from far away, but it was known the world over that this was of no help whatsoever. The Sirens' melody permeated everything, even wax, and the longings of those they seduced, would shatter heftier bonds than chain and mast.

Odysseus did not ponder upon it even though he had in all likelihood heard about it. He thoroughly trusted his handful of wax and length of chain, and with innocent contentment in his unorthodox strategy, journeyed forth to encounter the Sirens.

The Sirens have yet another weapon, even more frightening than their melody, that of their silence. Admittedly, this has not so far taken place, but it is not at all unthinkable, that someone who has been redeemed from the grip of their song, could most definitely not be rescued from their silence. No earthly power can resist the thrill of vanquishing them in one's own right, and the ensuing overwhelming arrogant pride.

Indeed, as Odysseus approached, the mighty songstresses did not sing; could it be that they thought this opponent would be defeated only by their silence, or could it be that the sight of total bliss on the face of Odysseus, who thought of nothing but wax and chain, made them forego their rapturous song?

Odysseus however, if one could so express it, did not hear their silence, he believed them to sing, though he was protected from it; he fleetingly saw the change in their throats, the deep breathing, the tearful eyes, and the half-parted lips. He thought they were arias that sounded without being heard; but soon all slipped away from his gaze into the distance, the Sirens simply vanished as he came closest to them, never to be heard again.

They however, lovelier than ever, turned with necks outstretched, letting their ghostly hair flutter free, scraped the rocks with their claws, for they no longer wanted to allure, but wished only to bathe in the brilliance emanating from the great eyes of Odysseus …for as long a time as possible. Had the Sirens possessed consciousness, they would be annihilated, but they lived on, only Odysseus evaded them.

There exists yet another codicil to this legend: Odysseus was so cunning a fox, that even the God of Destiny could not permeate his inner self; perhaps he had actually realised that the Sirens had remained silent and he had held up to them and to the Gods, a pretentious demeanour merely as a shield, although that is beyond the grasp of the human mind.

INTERPRETATION

Kafka's literary vessel now journeys through dangerous waters… accompanying Odysseus on his legendary travels as he confronts the singing Sirens. Mythology says that Odysseus, instructed by the enchantress Circe, had his crew plug their ears with wax and tie him to his ship's mast, as he sailed through the Sirens' domain; when the enchantment of their song took hold… Odysseus struggled to be freed, forcing his crew to secure him further, and so ensuring his safe passage onwards. One may wonder what inspiration Kafka gained from the king of Ithaca, Odysseus the cunning, also known as Ulysses: Is it possible that Kafka compared his literary odyssey to that of the great Ulysses and his adventurous journeys? Ironically, Kafka's literature appears to possess close parallels with Odysseus' famous Trojan Horse: Superficially, both appear to be nothing more than an impressive inanimate ornament, a gift to the unsuspecting recipient; but hidden deep within, a ferocious army with purpose, primed to invade at the heart of our existence, seizing control of our complacent lives!

By means of wax and chain ...Odysseus submitted to the simplest measures before sailing forth to confront the Sirens, so as to deafen his crew and restrain himself from temptation. Indeed such simple measures – some might even say 'childish' – can provide the most adequate protection when facing the gravest danger. Could this be Kafka's admission that the simplest measures served him well enough? Since he published so little of his work in his lifetime, it is feasible that Kafka considered the critics of his work to be his Sirens; armed with their critical song ...and capable of alluring any writer who dares sail through their literary seas; it would be easier for Kafka to deafen himself to any such critical song by keeping most of his work unpublished, thus securing himself firmly to his literary mast for protection. Though any traveller could have used the same means as Odysseus for self-preservation, this would have been of no benefit to them; for the Sirens' melody can penetrate any such wax, forcing those enchanted to break even the strongest chains. Did Kafka believe that other writers could have undertaken the same precautions as himself, limiting the amount of work they published so as to save themselves from the critical song? Such condemnation can often be so crushing to a writer's creative flow. However, many writers are so easily enticed by the song of their Sirens... that they can all too quickly break the bonds of their literary chain and mast.

Odysseus utterly trusted his measures of protection, and ventured forth with absolute contentment. The Sirens however, chose a more dangerous weapon than their song ...their silence: These Songstresses have never remained silent before, and though one might hope to be rescued from their melody ...from their silence certainly never; but the thought of being able to reprieve oneself – and in so doing vanquish the Sirens – is a delightful prospect. Kafka may have joyously proceeded with his strategy in dealing with potential critics, but felt unprepared for a silent response to the few pieces of work he had published. Any criticism would allow the author an opportunity to respond, but without a censorious voice it would be impossible to know how his work had been received. A writer could certainly redeem himself from the song of his Sirens, but would be unable to save himself from the torment of their silence… though reprieve from these perils would inspire great pride. As Odysseus approached, the Sirens remained silent, whether they believed that their silence alone was enough to annihilate this legendary adversary, or that the contentment that shone from Odysseus' face had stunned them into silence…is unknown. Did Kafka feel the critics believed, that by not commenting on his work they would steer him into oblivion, or was he more hopeful, that the radiance shining from his literary truth had stunned them into silence?

Odysseus was unaware of the Sirens' silence, though he believed he heard their captivating song… the briefest glimpse convincing him that they were in the midst of singing; this moment passed just as quickly as it arrived, for Odysseus was now gone, well beyond the domain of the enchanting song-stresses, never to hear them again: A possible admission by Kafka that despite the absence of criticism, he believed he heard those critical voices lambasting his work so clearly; his time in the limelight passing as quickly as it arrived, he now disappeared into his distant literary horizon, far beyond the realms of his critics. The Sirens, now turning with outstretched necks and flowing hair, no longer wished to allure Odysseus, instead desired only to bask in the brilliance that radiated from his great eyes; had the Sirens been aware that they themselves were allured by Odysseus, they would have been vanquished; instead, they lived on… unable to destroy this man with his armour of wax and chain. Did Kafka now believe that

32

with him publishing no further work, his critics longed for more, only wishing to continually bathe in his literary brilliance? Any such critics would be vanquished if they understood his work and recognised the meaning within, for there would be no need for censure.

The legend adds, that Odysseus was so full of guile that even Destiny itself could not pierce his self-belief; that he was aware of the Sirens' silence all along, but acted out a pretence, merely to protect himself from the gods …though nobody can be sure of this. This may be a tantalising admission from Kafka himself, that his concerns over the effects of any such criticism was purely a pretence, undertaken for the purpose of appeasing his literary god …his truth, and so maintaining his acute style!

The example of Odysseus is a lesson to behold, for when our Sirens begin to sing… trying to enchant us with their song, or should they even remain silent…in hope that we will imagine the worst, we should arm ourselves with our own metaphorical ball of wax and length of chain: Only by deafening ourselves to such unnecessary critical song, and securing ourselves to the mast of our truth, can we focus on the destination ahead …and sail on by!

THE SILENCE OF THE SIRENS

Enchanted song-stresses with veiled melody, lure Ulysses forth to a grave in the sea

Beautiful music... over waters he sails, masking the perils his journey entails

Curious rapture... intriguing to hear, crushing all doubt whilst relinquishing fear

Captivated by rhapsody... so bound to please, gave into temptation ...the brave Ulysses

Chained to his Mast... held firm in his place, the crew thus instructed for him they must brace

A handful of wax used to deafen each man, so no one will falter from entrusted plan

As his ship sails on by with strategic intent, The Sirens' intentions begin to relent

Held firm to his vessel... thus resisting ill fate, the sea-mistresses' plan has been all but too late

Revelling in radiance of determined success, the defeated Sirens...soothed by radiant caress

Victorious Ulysses accomplished in mission, drowned are the efforts of death's apparition

*What lesson is taught from this insightful tale, our awareness
to danger we must always avail!*

*In times when we're lured into ill consequence, let us be
chained to our mast and hold courage immense*

*And have our crew of emotions maintaining their course, so the
wrong choice of action won't cause us remorse*

*So we freely sail by...onto our destination, and rejoice in the
resplendence of our liberation!*

ON THE QUESTION OF LAWS

Our laws are unfortunately unknown by the general public, they are kept a secret by the small circle of the nobility who rules over us. We are convinced that these ancient laws are meticulously applied; regardless, it is still extremely distressing to be controlled by laws that one does not know. I am not thinking about the variance in interpretation and the disadvantages that are brought about when only a few individuals and not the whole nation are allowed to partake in the administration of the Law. These disadvantages are perhaps of no importance at all. The laws are indeed ancient and have been subject to interpretation for hundreds of years, even those renditions have doubtless been already turned into laws; admittedly there exists some freedom of interpretation, albeit restricted, that persists to this day. Moreover, the aristocracy has evidently no reason to be influenced in its interpretation by its personal interests ...that would be to our disadvantage; for from the beginning, laws have been set and designed for the noblemen who remain above them, which is why the Law exists exclusively in their control. Naturally, there is wisdom in this – who would challenge the wisdom of this time-served Law? But it is likely an ordeal for us ...that is probably inevitable.

Incidentally, these contrived laws could actually be a matter of conjecture. There is a tradition that they endure and have been entrusted as a secret to the aristocracy, but that is and can be nothing more than an ancient tradition, credible only thanks to its antiquity; for by their nature, these laws require that their holders keep its secrecy. When some amongst the people follow the actions of the nobility vigilantly, along with the records our forefathers and ourselves have continued to conscientiously accumulate about them, and when we believe to recognize in innumerable facts, certain guidelines for whatever legal provision, and when we try to adjust ourselves a little to our present and future according to these thoroughly sifted and reordered inferences – all then appears highly uncertain and even a play of the mind, for perhaps these laws that we are trying to untangle, do not exist at all. There is a small faction that is really of this opinion and tries to establish that: The Law is whatever the aristocracy does. This faction sees only the arbitrary actions of the nobility and discards the people's tradition, which according to their opinion only brings minor occasional benefits but mostly grave drawbacks, for it gives the people a false and treacherous certainty bordering on recklessness – regarding forthcoming events. This harm is not to be denied but the absolute majority of our people trust the cause to be the inadequacy of tradition… which should be more thoroughly delved into; the material certainly appears immense to us, yet it is too measly and it will still take hundreds of years before it is adequate and satisfactory. The present bleakness of this outlook is only brightened by the belief that there will come a time when the tradition and its scholarship shall reach the conclusion, virtually with a sigh of relief, that everything is clear, that the Law now belongs to the people, and the aristocracy vanishes. This is not uttered with any hatred against the aristocracy, definitely not and by no one; we instead rather hate ourselves, for we cannot yet be worthy of the Law. In a sense this is the reason why the alluring party that does not believe in any true and effective law, has remained so small, for it has also unequivocally acknowledged the nobility and its right to exist. Actually, this could only be expressed through a paradox: Any party that would discard both the belief in the laws and the nobility, would immediately have the support of the entire population, but such a party cannot emerge while no one dares to abolish the nobility. We live on this razor's edge. A writer had once so summarised: The sole conspicuous unquestionable Law that is imposed on us is the nobility, and should we cheat ourselves out of this only Law?

INTERPRETATION

Although the Laws of our Land rule our everyday lives, how often do we seriously consider this imposed system of order? All who are confined within the parameters of the Law should delve into its origins, question the effect of its enforcement as it strives to maintain order, and contemplate the journey it has taken to arrive where it stands today. It is with this in mind that an advocate of both Law and Literature, Franz Kafka, has undertaken this – so often overlooked, but nonetheless vital – task of enlightenment: For who is better equipped to illuminate the complexities of the Law, along with the quandary society faces, both in its simplest terms and at its deepest level, than the great Kafka himself?

Kafka writes that the Law is not known by the general population, it is instead a secret held by the ruling classes; and despite believing that laws are applied fastidiously, it can be a most unpleasant experience to be forced to live under rules that we do not comprehend. Kafka's opening verses epitomise our system of governance; though the majority of people may believe the Law is implemented fairly and meticulously, in reality, it is applied at the will of the Authorities and remains a mystery to all except them: For the general population's faithful obedience of these time-served laws is probably more a consequence of ignorance, rather than a genuine trust in the system and its advocates; which is why Kafka remarks that it is extremely distressing to be ruled by laws one does not know. He is not preoccupied with the occasional discrepancies in the Law's interpretation, nor with the shortcomings that arise when only a small group is charged with its administration: For these drawbacks may bear no significance at all; discrepancies are bound to occur in a system as vastly complex as the Law, and it is therefore understandable that only a small group of individuals – with the adequate wisdom and academic knowledge – should be charged with its control. Kafka appreciates that the Law's development has been the result of many years of interpretation, alteration and application, and has thus evolved to a point where it serves adequately for now, but there is and always will be minor scope for improvements. Kafka's objectivity views the Law in its entirety, instead of on the merits of individual cases where it may have been misinterpreted…much to the disadvantage of the individual who suffers unjustly: For regardless of such injustices, it is the correct and fair administration of the Law that matters in general.

Kafka acknowledges that the ruling classes have no obvious reason to deliberately interpret the Law to the disadvantage of the masses – though the evidence suggests otherwise! – for laws were developed from the very beginning by the ruling classes for their benefit alone, which is why they stand above them and continue to maintain control. It is indeed understandable, that the very small percentage of society who possesses the most…should want to protect itself from the greater population that possesses the least. Though there may be wisdom in the word of the Law, as these enduring rules have served throughout many generations – dutifully followed by most – it can so often become an overbearing and inevitable ordeal to endure. Kafka concedes that these laws may actually have no solid basis whatsoever, but are instead an illusion made to appear real. This reveals how fragile the system of Law is; for it is not a physical force holding the people in place, but a psychological instrument planted in the mind, solely dependent on unquestionable compliance. As the old generations pass on and new ones arrive… they continue to conform to this perpetually controlling system: How vital it is for those who control the Law to keep its essence a mystery – since the Law only consists of written codes of conduct passed down by customary ethical instruction – so its illusionary power continues to reign, as well as demand respect!

Kafka speaks of those who strive to keep records on the actions of the ruling classes and their forefathers, using accumulated data to unravel the mysteries of the Law and its administration. Though these people believe they identify discrepancies that assist them to adjust their lives accordingly, they find themselves bewildered when they try... for the Law itself is in fact nothing more than a complicated imaginary system designed and applied for the benefit of the ruling classes. Kafka appreciates that there will always be those who question the rule of authority, but recognises that despite the discrepancies they note, and the efforts they may make to circumvent the Law's control, this turns out to be futile, for the Law is altered at the will of the upper classes. He then turns his attention to an even smaller group of people who may be the most enlightened of all, as they recognise that the Law is whatever the ruling classes do: This small group sees the acts of the Law as only whimsical, applied conditionally to satisfy the needs and wants of its authority; moreover it holds no faith in the old traditions, as it believes these customs will require considerably more time and deliberation before developing into a reliable structured system to follow: These outdated traditions are of little benefit to the people in the long-term, for they make them ill prepared for dealing with an uncertain and changeable future. This enlightened small group appears to be caught in a somewhat daunting dilemma, for it sees the Law as a manipulative tool of authority, whilst also recognising tradition as an unstructured inherited routine... so in what middle-ground could one find the solution?

Kafka notes that there is a light of hope in the darkness of this current condition, when the people's tradition, along with their academic understanding, will evolve to a degree that allows the Law to become theirs... leading to the disappearance of the ruling classes. However, he believes the general population is at present unprepared to be entrusted with control of the Law, and it would be of no use to deliberately eliminate the rule of authority ...just yet; this is why the masses are more inclined to hate themselves rather than the ruling classes. Perhaps it is this very self-loathing that is responsible for the all too frequently disruptive, even somewhat anarchistic behaviour that ironically justifies the control that the Authorities exert. It appears that many hold at least a mild form of contempt for a system that dictates and restricts, as well as for the guardians who enforce it; though the people may willingly support the removal of this system…what would be the consequences? Kafka highlights the necessity for the upper classes' control over the Law, for without these rulers to maintain such standards of conduct and civility… what would the general population aspire to?

Where religion and tradition once dictated the order of the day, evolution and diversity in modern day society now demand applicable rules of guidance and discipline so all can be governed fairly. The ruling classes that once created the initial structure have now evolved into the establishment that has taken charge: If we ponder *On the question of Laws* we come to realise that the establishment must exist so as to maintain the order that the general population cannot maintain for itself. Though Kafka appears to support the rule of authority, condemning the masses to suppression and exploitation by an apparently cruel and self-serving master …his tale should be considered thoughtfully, for it illustrates that if the people wish to have the power of authority, they must demonstrate enough authority over themselves to be given the power, ultimately transforming their condition from those who are ruled…to those who are rulers!

A FRATRICIDE

It is proven that the murder took place in the following manner:

Schmar, the murderer, positioned himself around nine o'clock, in the moonlit night, at the corner where, Wese, the victim, came out of his office and had to turn into the street where he lived.

The icy evening air was dead cold. Schmar had only a light blue shirt on; moreover, it was unbuttoned. He did not shiver but was of course moving all the time. He held the bare murder weapon, half bayonet, half kitchen knife firmly in his grip. He studied the cutting edge against the moonlight; it was gleaming; though not enough for Schmar; he struck it against the pavement bricks until there were sparks; perhaps he already regretted this; and perhaps to make up for the damage, he stroked the blade against the sole of his boot, as if it were a violin bow; at the same time, standing on one leg and leaning forward, he listened to the knife drawing across his boot sole; the sound reverberated in the fateful side street.

Why did Pallas, the private civilian who from his second floor window had witnessed everything, tolerate it? Fathom the mysteries of human nature! With his collar turned up, his nightgown tied firmly around his ample body, he glanced down, shaking his head.

Five houses further down, diagonally opposite him, there was Mrs. Wese, in her nightgown and wrapped up in fox fur, looking out for her husband who was uncharacteristically late today.

At last, there rings the doorbell outside Wese's office, a sound too loud for a doorbell, over the town and up toward the sky, and Wese, the diligent night shift worker, steps out of the house into the street, still uncertain, heralded only by the sound of the bell; the pavement starts at once marking off his silent steps.

Pallas bends far forward; he ought not miss anything. Mrs.Wese, now serene for having heard the bell, shuts her rattling

43

windowpanes. Schmar kneels down; he presses his face and hands against the pavement stones, for he has no other exposed parts of his body; everything else is freezing, whereas Schmar blazes.

Just at the intersection, where the lanes divide, there stands Wese, propping himself up in the street beyond with only the aid of a walking cane. A whim. The night sky, dark blue and golden, has lured him. Unwittingly he looks on; unaware, he raises his hat and strokes his hair beneath; nothing up there bodes ill, nothing to indicate the very next hereafter; everything remains in its nonsensical, unventured place. It is in itself quite reasonable that Wese should walk further ...but he walks right into Schmar's knife.

'Wese!' cries out Schmar, standing on tiptoe, the arm outstretched, the knife sharply lowered, 'Wese! Julia is waiting in vain' ...and Schmar stabs, right into the throat and left into the throat and the third time, deep into the belly. Slashed water rats do not let out as loud a wail as Wese.

'Done', says Schmar as he hurls the knife away, that superfluous blood stained ballast against the front wall of the nearest house. The bliss of murder! The relief, the ecstasy in shedding foreign blood! Wese, old night raven, friend, alehouse comrade, seeping away into the dark ground of the street. Why are you not simply a blood filled balloon, so that I could burst you and make you vanish completely. Not all wishes become fulfilled, not all flourishing dreams ripen, your hefty remains lie here, already unresponsive to every kick. Thereby what is the point of the soundless query you may have?

Pallas, choking on the venom in his body, stands at his double winged opened house door. 'Schmar! Schmar! Everything noted, nothing overlooked.' Pallas and Schmar scrutinise one another. Pallas is gratified, Schmar comes to no conclusion.

Mrs.Wese, the crowd by her sides, her face aged by horror, hurries over. The fur coat swings open, she hurls herself over

Wese; the nightgown clad body belongs to him, the fur, spreading over the wedded couple, just like the turf over a grave, belongs to the crowd.

Schmar, curbing his nausea with difficulty, presses his lips against the shoulder of the policeman, who stepping lightly ...leads him away.

INTERPRETATION

Kafka now ventures into the darker side of human nature to elucidate the fatal consequences of one man's murderous action, another man's bloodthirsty inaction, resulting in the brutal – and wholly unnecessary – death of an unsuspecting victim, and a great loss to a loving loyal spouse. Though one's attention may be drawn to the murderer and victim, the witness to the crime and the dutiful wife also play an equally important role, as the lives of all become affected by this single event.

Kafka outlines Schmar's every chilling action in the freezing night air, exposing the burning hatred that fuels his vengeful lust, as he prepares for the fateful moment ahead; Kafka introduces Wese, the victim who makes his way home through the still, silent evening, unaware of what lies in wait for him; to follow on is Pallas, the voyeuristic witness whose curiosity renders him helpless, allowing the inevitable to materialise before his eyes; finally, Wese's wife is brought into the tale, dutifully waiting for a husband who will never arrive home. Kafka may not only be illustrating the consequence of action and inaction, but through the title of A Fratricide he highlights the cause and effect of such acts of inhumanity on mankind's brotherly bond.

When Schmar executed his homicidal plan, he became responsible for committing a duel murder: The obvious physical kill of Wese, followed by the metaphorical death of Mr and Mrs

Wese' life together. The implications of this act were not only the loss of life to a man, but also the loss of a loved husband to a wife, as well as a precious son to his parents, a valued brother to his siblings, an appreciated friend to his colleagues, and a vital contributor to society. Though the reader's attention may well be focused on Schmar, it is actually Pallas the Observer that holds the greatest position of power. From his elevated vantage point Pallas witnessed the spine-chilling scene before him, as he remained hidden in the shadows watching Schmar preparing for the attack …with murderous intent in every gesture. With only a turn of his head, Pallas could see the unsuspecting Wese stroll ever closer to his tragic fate, oblivious to the danger that lay ahead. Then Pallas, with a casual look in opposite direction, would find Mrs. Wese, eagerly awaiting her husband's return home, thoroughly unaware of how her life would change very shortly, forever. Pallas held within his grasp, the power to call attention to Schmar's disturbing behaviour, thus preventing him from committing this dastardly act, and so turning him into a murderer; the guilt of which he would never be able to remove from his conscience. Pallas had the opportunity to make Wese aware of the danger ahead, and so deter him from walking into the brutal attack that would rob him of his life and love. Pallas failed to act to protect Mrs. Wese, and give her the chance to save both her husband and Schmar from an unnecessary fate. Pallas' inaction may well have resulted in him committing a triple fratricide, allowing the death of Wese, the damnation of Schmar and the great loss to Mrs. Wese. He could have warned all concerned …but chose to do nothing, Pallas surely damned himself to a sentence of guilt and regret. The power over three lives rested in his hands at that moment in time, and he chose death and tragedy for his two brothers and sister… instead of the right course of action.

So why does Pallas stand idly by? What motive could have driven him to remain silent? Where was his compassion when the moment called for it? What possible reason would a man have to allow a clearly preventable act of inhumanity? The morbid curiosity that appears to lie at the heart of the human psyche, where those horrors one flees in times of danger, become all too compelling to miss when one is positioned safely at a distance! But for Pallas – and others who follow his example – the price he may ultimately pay for such bloodlust will be the guilt that will disturb his waking moments …and bring him nightmares whilst he sleeps.

It is also conceivable that Kafka used A Fratricide to illustrate how he viewed himself in relation to the literary fraternity: Kafka may have considered himself similar to Pallas the witness, whose morbid curiosity and voyeuristic nature compels him to stand in the shadows and allow such horrors to take place, only to remark on them once the deed is done. Kafka may have thought of Schmar the murderer as the critics, these dark and dangerous characters who lurk in the back alleys of the literary world, preparing themselves to pounce on their unsuspecting victims… ruthlessly burying their sharpened scornful criticisms into the work of their prey. Kafka may identify other authors with Wese the night-worker, hard-working and devoted, working long into the night, contributing honestly and importantly to society, only to finish their work, pause at the crossroads of success and have the critics leap out and attack them. Kafka may believe the loyal reading audience to be akin to Mrs. Wese, eagerly awaiting their favourite authors returning to them after being locked away producing the fruits of their labour, only to find these authors destroyed at the hands of the critics. Perhaps Kafka considered his literary circle as a fraternity, a brotherhood of writers, with an important relation to both readers and critics alike; and though constructive criticism may have been valued, Kafka may have considered unnecessary criticism as almost a homicide, and one which he could nothing against but stand by and observe, merely noting the outcome!

The story of A Fratricide may offer a word of caution and a lesson in life, that inaction is as powerful as action itself. Whatever one chooses to do, or not do... as the case may be, could have far reaching consequences, for all involved. Shall we stand idly by when we possess the power of choice and do nothing? Or should we use our virtue and liberate others, as well as ourselves ...from the darker side of humanity?

THE PASSENGER

I stand on the platform of the streetcar, totally uncertain about my station in this world, in this city, in my family. Not even casually could I rightly express my claims and desires in whatever direction. I have no defence to offer at all for standing on this platform, holding onto the strap, letting the streetcar carry me along; nor for the people who dodge this vehicle or silently stroll on by... or stand still before shop windows. No one of course demands that from me, but that is immaterial.

The streetcar approaches a stop; a young lady is standing next to the steps, ready to alight. I can see her so clearly, as if I had felt her with my fingers. She is dressed in black, the pleats of her skirt hardly move, her blouse is tight fitting, with a white, finely stitched lace collar, her left hand lays flat on the side of the tram and the umbrella in her right hand rests on the second highest step. Her face is brown, the nose, slightly pinched on the sides, seems round and wide. She has lots of brown hair and tiny stray curls on her right temple. Her little ear is close-set, and I can even see the right ear muscle and the shadow at the root, for I am sitting so close.

I asked myself at the time: How is it, that she is not amazed at herself, that she keeps her mouth closed and does not speak of such things?

INTERPRETATION

The journey of life rolls forward, continually evolving, constantly in motion ...inadvertently carrying us along with it! We are all merely passengers on this ride, our place defined by who we are, the scenery along the way forever changing...the destination unsure, for it is the driver of this vehicle who chooses the course and journey's end …this driver is *Fate*! Does Kafka recognise that he too is merely a passenger riding on life's carriage, uncertain of where he should stand, of the journey ahead, of even the choices he must make? He acknowledges being only a vigilant observer who closely studies those sharing the journey with him… as well as those whom he passes along the way.

The narrator admits he feels uncertain of his position within his family, within the city he calls home, and even the world as he knows it… whilst he stands on the platform of this vehicle. Could Kafka concede that he too feels uncertain of his standing in life, unsure of his rightful place within his family, unsure of his standing within the city he knows so well, and unsure of even his footing within the world as he knows it? The despairing and unconventional nature of Kafka's work reflects a mind-set that appears to function outside the realms of popular opinion…thus banishing him into a somewhat isolated existence. The narrator is unable to choose any particular direction to satisfy his beliefs or desires; he offers no defence for where he stands on the street car's platform, holding onto the strap whilst carried along; even those he passes along the way, leave him bewildered as to why they are there. Is this Kafka's admission that he feels uncertain of the rightful direction he should take in life, unsure of which road to follow in order to confirm his beliefs or fulfil his desires? And, at the same time, does he also feel unable to find answers for why Fate has placed him on the platform of Destiny's vehicle, where all he can do is steady himself by holding onto his metaphorical strap – his literature – as he is inadvertently carried along? Kafka may consider himself, as well as others, to be nothing but instruments of Fate! No one seeks an explanation from him… this is immaterial, for it is his own curiosity that inspires such questions, compelling him to search for answers.

The narrator is aware of the streetcar approaching a stop, whereupon a young lady is preparing to disembark; he recognises certain aspects of her so very distinctly, observing in such detail her attire as well as the most intricate curves and lines of her features ...as if he had physically caressed each observance for affirmation; he finds himself amazed by her composure, how she remains silent instead of speaking of the wonderment he sees in her. Here Kafka's attention to detail becomes evident, so precise... and yet at times, so confusing and apparently irrelevant, those details that appear so note-worthy to him, passing unnoticed to others who obliviously pass by. Perhaps this reveals Kafka's close scrutiny of other writers ...as they ride along their literary journey: His close observation of their style, subject matter and presentation, as they prepare to alight at the point of publication, amazed by their literary contribution and how comfortable they feel publishing their work, unlike himself who published so little. Unfortunately for Kafka, it appears his streetcar terminated far too early...for illness forced him to alight far too early!

As we are carried along life's path on destiny's carriage, we may feel uncertain of our place or the direction we should take; we may often question the position we hold and the purpose we serve, and may also regularly contemplate, with much trepidation, what lies ahead and where this journey will end! We can take comfort in the knowledge that others will share the same predicament; though there will be times on this adventure when we may nervously struggle to maintain our balance, let self-confidence be the strap we hold onto to steady ourselves for the road ahead, so that we can enjoy the scenery along the way, in anticipation of the destination, as Fate carries us forward ...sticking rigidly to its timetable!

THE PASSENGER

My place in life I must define… I'm in search of who I am
So I climb aboard and take my seat… for the journey on
Destiny's Tram

With a style unique I'm one of a kind… reflecting insightful
flair
I sit at the back, others the middle and front… Creativity's my
bill of fare

Whilst carried along this uncertain road… contemplating my
destination
A girl steadies herself and prepares to alight… as I consider
this implication

She holds onto the strap to maintain her balance… her detail
finitely clear
I notice the things that others don't see… from her clothes to
the style of her hair

Now I do not profess to know how this all ends… or of the
scenery along the way
But a great leap of faith is on what it depends… as I travel this
path here today

Be sure to carefully choose the position you take… and how
you arrive at your choices
Else it may all end in a costly mistake… when your words
become lost in strange voices

THE NEW ADVOCATE

We have a new advocate, Dr. Bucephalus. There is little in his appearance to remind of the time, when he was indeed Alexander of Macedonia's battle steed. Plenty is however noticeable by whomever is familiar with such circumstances. Recently, I saw on a flight of stairs, a quite unsophisticated usher whose appearance reflected only that of those regular patrons at the races, gazing at the advocate with admiration, as he climbed up, heaving his shanks, the sound of his every step echoing on the marble.

In the main, the Bar sanctions the admission of Bucephalus. With astounding insight, one accepts that Bucephalus is in a difficult place by today's social standards, and considering his historical station and significance to the world, he merits a degree of goodwill. Today – and that cannot be denied – there is not another Great Alexander. To be sure, there are plenty who know how to murder; and there is no lack of dexterity in lunging at a friend across the banquet table, with a lance; and for many Macedonia is too confined, so that they curse Philip the father – but no one, no one can lead the way to India. Already in the past, the gateways of India were unreachable, yet the path was signalled by the sword of the king. Today the goals are elsewhere, farther and loftier; no one points the way; there are many who carry swords, but only so that they could brandish them ceremoniously; and thus they confuse the gaze of he who wishes to follow them.

It is perhaps truly for the best, to immerse oneself in the books of Law, just as Bucephalus has done. Free, his flanks unhampered by the riders' loins, in the subdued lamplight, far from the rages of Alexander's blood-drenched battlefields, he reads and turns the pages of our ancient scripts.

INTERPRETATION

Bucephalus, the mighty battle steed of Alexander the Great takes centre stage, as Kafka now transforms this old advocate of history into *The New Advocate* of Law. It is somewhat puzzling to see where Kafka finds his inspiration from this legendary horse, but the significance of Bucephalus may lie in the role he played rather than who he was: This magnificent steed was responsible for carrying the man who created a great historical legacy, therefore… Bucephalus literally carried history forward. One of Alexander's most trusted companions, Bucephalus was considered by some as his closest friend, accompanying him on many exploits, advancing his master to great victories, thus playing a vital role in how history was sculpted; but he always remained a dutiful servant directed by the hand of Alexander, and unlike the great man himself, did so without the desire for gain or glory! With *The New Advocate*, Kafka appears to highlight the need to involve history's rich experience within modern day Law.

Bucephalus was bred from the best Thessalonian strain and christened so because his head was as broad as a bull's, hence its literal meaning 'Ox-headed'. Alexander was only a boy when he encountered Bucephalus, taming the beast so he could mount him… and in doing so… impressing his father Philip II, who is reported to have said 'O my son, look thee a kingdom equal to and worthy of thyself, for Macedonia is too little for thee'. It is unsure whether Bucephalus died of old age or battle wounds, but Alexander buried him in Jalapar Sharif, outside Jhelum, Pakistan, naming the city Bucephala in the horse's honour.

The new advocate, Dr. Bucephalus… arrives at the Law; though his appearance has changed much since his great days with Alexander, those who are familiar with his circumstances appreciate his reputation. Does Kafka suggest that the reputation of the once iconic figures of history will eventually fade in the minds of successive generations? The passing of time will relegate these figures to only memory, and eventually written record... regardless of their achievements and contributions. Despite Bucephalus' demeanour, he holds a presence noticeable to even the least worldly of people, who cast an admiring eye upon this new advocate; how the distinctive qualities of great historical characters still hold a mysterious allure instinctively recognised and admired by others, irrespective of their social standing or intellect!

The consensus of the Bar is that they approve of Dr. Bucephalus' appointment, though one requires enough insight to recognise the difficult position he finds himself in, as the modern society he now integrates into, is far different from the one where his master reigned supreme; regardless of this predicament, his achievements and reputation command at the very least ...some degree of respect. Do these lines echo Kafka's beliefs on the Law... that those involved in shaping History in a different era – who become advocates of modern Law – are in a difficult position? One requires enough insight to recognise the achievements of these historical figures, who must play a role in the formulation of modern day Law. Though today's society enjoys a more secure, comfortable and civilised existence than those ruled by the war-mongering conquerors of the past, structure and governance must be forged with wisdom in mind; for it is the actions of those from the past, that have been instrumental in shaping their tomorrow, which has become ...our today!

It cannot be denied that no one could be compared to Alexander the Great in our present era, though many know how to take a life ...with no skill nor courage required, solely for the act of doing so; despite this, such people find Macedonia too limiting, and so curse Alexander's father Philip... for they are unable to lead the way to India themselves. Is Kafka suggesting that there are no longer great characters to add to the ledgers of history? No more great conquerors to wage war and fight legendary battles ...building monumental empires in their name? Though it is easy to behave in an uncivilised manner in a civilised environment, to bring civility to the uncivilised requires greatness. Maybe those who find Macedonia too confining find their own small existence too limiting, but... with no distant empires to be conquered they must surely curse Philip; for he pointed the way for Alexander, so no others need follow. Kafka appears to acknowledge that much of the world is conquered, and there is very little left for man to conquer ...but himself; no one points the way because no one needs to point the way... empires no longer exist to be won or lost. Today, it is the word of Law, not the sword of legendary conquerors that govern our lives: Though nowadays many carry swords, they only do so as decoration, brandishing them as a feeble gesture, without conviction, confusing those who follow them. Swords no longer need to be used, and so become nothing more than ornaments of authority ...instead of instruments of purpose; such actions only confuse those who look on, awaiting their use with conviction or justification; without this intention ...why carry them at all?

The story concludes... it may be best to focus our studies on the Law, just as Bucephalus has done; for now he is free and far away from the war-torn battlefields, he settles calmly beneath the lamplight studying the ancient scripts. Kafka may concede...that the time of those great characters who built empires has passed, and though history's contribution in shaping our civilised society has been vital, modern-day Law must now take precedence. However, if we truly wish to honour and cherish the precious Law we live by, we must use the wisdom and guidance of those who have fought to bring civility to our lives.

REFLECTIONS FOR
GENTLEMEN-JOCKEYS

When you think about it, nothing can lure one to be the winner in a race.

The glory of being acknowledged as the best rider in the land by the kick-off of the band, delights too much not to bring on remorse, the morning after.

The envy of the rivals, of the cunning and of the influential people, must wound us in the narrow course that we are crossing in order to reach the plain which will shortly remain empty before us, save for a few lapping racers who start riding on the edge of the horizon.

Many of our friends hurry to raise their winnings and shout "hurrahs" only over their shoulders, from remote pay boxes; our best friends however, have not bet at all on our horse, for they feared that if it led to losses, they would have to be cross with us; but now that our horse is the winner and they have not won anything, they turn away as we come close and prefer to look towards the stands.

The competitors behind us, firmly in the saddle, try to ignore the disgrace that has befallen them and the injustice they have suffered; they adopt a fresh outlook, as if they were to start a new race and a serious one at that...after this mere child's play.

To many women the winner cuts a ridiculous figure, for he is inflated and indeed awkward with the never-ending handshakes, greetings, bowing and waving, while the defeated shut their mouths and casually pat their neighing horses on the neck.

Finally, it begins to rain from the cloudy sky.

INTERPRETATION

The Winner's predicament …unimaginable to any spectator who sees only the joyous celebrations for the illustrious champion, as he is carried along on the wave of euphoria! Who could imagine a more intoxicating prospect than success? The prospect of overcoming all others …including the odds, so as to be first past the post; the prospect of rising to the challenge of competition, so as to be crowned the best in one's endeavours; but could any winner imagine the feelings their victory incites in others, whose negative or insincere reactions can surprise even the most experienced in human understanding: Using *Reflections of Gentlemen Jockeys* Kafka removes the nostalgic romanticism from the euphoria of winning, presenting a somewhat cynical but none-the-less realistic picture of all who share in just one person's moment of glory.

The parable illustrates the false enthusiasm of well wishers, whose faith in the winner's success is inspired only by the profits they claim from their crafty wagers, shouting insincere "Hurrahs" over their shoulders as they rush to collect their fortunate gains… for his success is their success! However, it is the winner's closest acquaintances who provoke the greatest disappointment, for they did not have enough faith in their dear friend to take a chance with even the smallest bet… at least as a spirited gesture; and so they must now turn away in disgust, disappointed that his victory has been their loss, bearing the underlying shame of their flagrant disloyalty.

The bitter jealousy of those rivals, begrudging the success of another, must haunt the winner as he turns back for a glance at his competitors: As selfish pride dictates their less than charitable reaction, their competitive nature prevents them from genuine acknowledgement. The defeated must now put on a brave show, pretending that this race was not important, convincing themselves that this was no competition but mere tomfoolery, a practice-run for a serious challenge to follow: How these people demonstrate such mastery in their field of expertise... but are no more than slaves to their egos!

The attention now turns to the winner, who can appear so preposterous under the watchful scrutiny of the ladies; with his overly inflated ego, along with a less than comfortable demeanour overwhelming him, as he takes centre stage... for now it is time to face the gauntlet of others who wish to take a share in his victorious moment; and all this takes place in front of the defeated who console themselves in silence, with half-hearted appreciation for their horses.

And now, the sunshine of this moment has gone, the rain of reality begins to fall, for the winner's time in the spotlight has quickly passed!

The well-deserved celebration for any winner becomes a battle to savour the victory: As jealousy and envy, hypocrisy and pretence, play their roles in the hearts of others who bear witness to this triumph. So when the moment of success arrives, and we ride our horse to victory, let us savour this fleeting chance to celebrate before the cloudy sky of other people's insincerity brings the raindrops of reality pouring down upon us!

GIVE IT UP!

It was very early in the morning, the streets were clean and clear, I was on my way to the railway station. As I compared the town clock with my wristwatch, I noticed it was much later than I had thought, I had to hurry; the horror of this discovery made me feel quite uncertain on my path, I did not yet know my way round this town very well, luckily there was a police constable nearby, I ran to him and breathlessly asked for directions. He smiled and said: "Do you want to find out the way from me?" 'Yes,' said I, 'for I cannot find it myself'. "Give it up, give it up!" he said and turned away with a sweeping motion, just like those who wish to be alone with their laughter.

INTERPRETATION

Give it up! ...could inspire most who read it to do exactly that, for there appears to be very little for the reader to contemplate: What modest substance there is, feels more like the account of an insignificant incident that one recalls in a passing conversation, and certainly not something worth wasting the ink of a literary master's pen! However, if one considers this piece from the perspective of the author, Kafka's own literary dilemma reveals itself: This short parable may have been inspired by the frustrations that forced Kafka on those occasions, when he was unable to settle into his writing, to reluctantly... *Give it up*!

The narrator mentions his early morning journey to the station, noting the immaculately deserted streets through which he ventures; Kafka may use this to illustrate his early morning journey, through the uncontaminated avenues of his mind... along which he has strolled so often, en route toward his literary station: The narrator's destination, from where he could board his literary train and be whisked away on whatever journey he wished, where neither time nor distance mattered, only the scenery and the much anticipated arrival. The narrator checked his wristwatch against the town's clock and discovered that he was behind in his time; this made him unsure of which route would serve him best ...for now he was forced to hurry. This may suggest that when Kafka's instinctive timing was out of synchronisation with the time he put aside for his writing, he became unsettled to such an extent that he was uncertain of how to proceed, as any discrepancy in his routine could have had disruptive consequences; furthermore, this would result in him feeling somewhat rushed, as he tried to make up for lost time.

The narrator admits he is unfamiliar with the town he is in, but fortunately sees a police constable, whom he approaches, so as to ask for directions. Is this Kafka's admission that he occasionally becomes lost as he tries to negotiate his mind's creative town, with its maze of avenues and myriad of choices? Despite this, he recognises his literary truth as the authoritative character from whom he can ask for directions. The constable appears surprised at the narrator's enquiry... for now he needs confirmation that he is being asked for help: The constable's only advice is to 'Give it up, give it up' ...and then he turns and walks away. Did Kafka believe his literary truth recognised that under these circumstances, when he was out of synchronisation and unsure of the right path, the best course of action would simply be to *Give it up* ...for now?!

Try as we may on occasion...to attend to that which we desire so greatly, circumstances will dictate whether we will be able to meet those goals, or whether it is best to resign ourselves to the situation and admit that there is no other alternative but to *Give it up!*

GIVE IT UP!

"Give it up" he said... "give it up" dear boy
For your desperate pursuit will bring you no joy

As I chase through the streets... in search of my station
My effort just brings me bemusing frustration

"Give it up" he said... "give it up" this time
There just isn't an answer to life's reason or rhyme

Though the need to fulfil my sacred routine
Is an honour of duty I've kept so pristine

"Give it up" he said... "give it up" my son
For it's time to concede that you've just missed this one

Behind in my timing... I've lost my direction
Reluctant surrender... may offer protection

"Give it up" he said... "give it up" for sure
Let go of this torment... be bothered no more

Though sometimes I'm lost as I strive to succeed
I must surrender the feeling of this desperate need

"Give it up" he said... "give it up" for now
For fate's intervention just will not allow

It's time to look for tomorrow... the new day that is dawning
And embrace every chance of this bright sunny morning

"Give it up" he said… "give it up" and be free
"Give it up" he said… "give it up" finally
If not for yourself… then for others and me
"Give it up"… dear boy… "give it up"!

POSEIDON

Poseidon sat at his desk and poured over the accounts of the oceans. The administration of the waters gave him endless work. He could have used assistants, as many as he wished, and of which he had so many, but since he took his task very seriously and checked everything down to the last penny, assistants were not going to be of much use to him. One could not say that he enjoyed the work, he carried it out merely because it was awarded to him; in fact he had often expressed his preference to apply for more cheerful jobs, but it became apparent that every time a different position was suggested, none appealed as much as his present post. It was therefore very difficult to find him another position. One could not possibly allocate a particular sea to him; quite apart from the fact that here... too the accounting job would not be smaller, only pettier, the great Poseidon could still always get an overriding post: Though if he were offered a position unrelated to the world's waters, he would feel sick, his divine breath would give into disorder, his chest would heave. In fact one did not take his troubles seriously; when a mighty person is tormented, one should seemingly abandon him to the hopelessness of his affairs. Nobody had really thought about relieving him from his post. He had been established as the God of the Seas from time immemorial and he was to remain there.

He got angriest – and this was the main source of his discontent with the job – when he heard the comments made about him, how he for instance rode forever over the tides, his Trident in hand. In the meantime he sat here in the depths of the world oceans and went over the accounts, uninterrupted; a trip to Jupiter now and then was the only disruption of the monotony, and by the way a journey from which he returned often more infuriated. He had barely seen the Seas, only cursorily on his hurried ascent to Mount Olympus ...and he had never really sailed over them. He cared to say that he awaited the sinking of the world, so that then, in a quiet moment, having thoroughly checked the final account, he could perhaps take a quick little tour.

INTERPRETATION

Poseidon, Greek mythology's god of the sea …is yet another character from the realms of myth and legend to arouse Kafka's imagination: However, instead of his usual depiction as the mighty ruler of the oceans, Kafka portrays him in a more sober light …as a discontented desk bound administrator trapped by destiny and duty. This appears to be yet another example of Kafka's acute perception, as he focuses on the day-to-day duties and difficulties even great gods must endure. Is it possible Kafka considered himself to endure the same predicament as Poseidon, toiling away in the depths of his literary ocean, trapped here by destiny, devoted to his duty?

Poseidon was most renowned as god of the seas, but was also the god of floods, droughts, earthquakes and horses: Generally portrayed as a mature man with a strong build and a dark beard holding a trident; he lived in a palace on the ocean floor made from coral and gems, and rode in a horse-drawn chariot. Poseidon could be a temperamental god; in a good mood he would create calm seas and new lands in the waters; when enraged, he would strike the ground with his trident causing earthquakes, shipwrecks and drowning.

The mighty Poseidon is confined to his desk, for the accounts of the waters are vast and their up-keep apparently endless; no amount of assistants could help with this task, for he…and he alone… must check every account to satisfy the vigour with which he attends to this duty. Here sits Kafka, confined to his bureau by his creative instincts, locked away in the depths of his literary ocean, an apparently endless stream of themes for his stories to be accounted for; a task which could only be served best by his devoted attendance, as no others could assist him with this mighty role. Though it is said that Poseidon did not enjoy this work, undertaking it because it was assigned to him, regardless of how many alternative positions he applied for... he could not perform a lesser duty than his present one; his credentials simply would not permit him to undertake a more trivial role than his demeanour dictated. The potential restlessness within Kafka's mind, a stirring discontent, challenged him on many occasions during his literary pursuits and occasionally made him desire a less demanding purpose, but always in his heart... he needed to perform this great and necessary duty: The author's demeanour unable to take on a more trivial writing style or limit the themes of his stories. Does Kafka admit that to perform a lesser task than that of his literary calling, only leaves him breathless and anxious at the very thought?

No one had taken Poseidon's troubles seriously, for his self-inflicted torment could only be resolved within his own mind, therefore, one had to leave him to dwell on the hopelessness of his affairs. The troubled mind of Franz Kafka, tormented by the questions of life's puzzles, is something he may have believed others did not take seriously, for only he was capable of finding answers to these quandaries: Could one contemplate relieving this mighty writer from his duties, an author whom fate had assigned to this station ...and one where he was to remain. The most infuriating aspects of Poseidon's work were the rumours circulating about him not taking his duties seriously, claiming he was spending his time cruising over the oceans brandishing his trident, as if only acting out his godly role: Instead, he was submerged beneath the fathoms of the oceans, in the depths of his work; his only opportunity to surface from his toil being the occasional journey to Jupiter, from which he often returned more infuriated. Is this a revelation by Kafka of his annoyance with those who believed he was not taking his literary work seriously, merely brandishing his pen as some kind of metaphorical trident which he held aloft whilst leisurely playing at being a writer? In reality, he was submerged in the depths of his literary ocean, scrupulously attending to his stories and parables with divine devotion; his only break from this monotonous duty was his ascent into the public realms, with the occasional publication; though such a journey may have caused greater frustration for him, with the reaction to his literature causing him to return to his writing duties in a more furious state.

Poseidon had hardly seen the oceans to which he devoted himself – and which he maintained so fastidiously – as he awaited the day when the world would sink and the last account would be filed...only then would he take a final little tour. Does Kafka conclude by suggesting that he never really had the opportunity to enjoy the work he maintained so conscientiously? But was instead awaiting the day when his creative productivity was no more, his time spent in isolation at an end, the last literary account filed, so that he could then take a final little tour of the public realms ...whilst sailing proudly over his literary seas!

Is the plight of Kafka's Poseidon so very different to the predicament of so many? For when one is locked away in the dedicated toil of one's duty, though there may be discontent with this role, resentment for the struggle, hope of change for more fulfilment, infuriating rumours, and little break from the monotony... one should not ascend into the heavens only to take fleeting glances back at what has been accomplished, awaiting the hopeful day when these achievements can finally be enjoyed!

POSEIDON

Within the depths of the oceans, engrossed in administration
Devoid of enjoyment, Poseidon felt no inspiration

Bound steady by his duty, this great god of the sea
Became chained by the will ...of his personal decree

Far down upon the seabed, in his palace of gems and corals
He toiled like a mortal, unable to rest upon his laurels

Discontented by this role he held, and in search of more
fulfilling
Very little was available, and what's been offered... he's not
willing

To do a lesser job's an insult, the task must match his might
Disturbed by such thoughts, he is overwhelmed with fright
.

But his devotion to his duty, doesn't show any resistance
For the scrutiny of the seas' accounts, is done with his
insistence

So complain he must... sharing his distress, unburdening his
frustration
Though all must pay attention and show respect... or stir his
agitation

Irritated by rumour... that his days are filled with pleasure
Though the endless focus on his task, gives no time for leisure

A fleeting glance is all he gets ...of the seas to which he tends

With a journey bound for Jupiter, up to Olympus he ascends

These occasional excursions… that this Titan must address
Moreover leave him furious, and adds to his distress

Waiting for the world to end, to make his final little tour
Of the waters that he rules so well, for they'll require him no
more

Could we learn from this example… of the great Poseidon's
plight?
To toil so hard and not enjoy the spoils, surely is not right!

Whether fate or luck has dealt its hand… to put us in this place
We should revel in the role we take… for it is destiny we face

So play your part and play it well… and aim to be divine
And be the best and love your role… and allow your life to
shine!

ELEVEN SONS

I have eleven sons.

The first is outwardly unappealing, but earnest and clever; nevertheless I cherish him, and though I love him as much as all my other children, I do not hold him in high esteem. It appears to me that his reasoning is too simple. He cannot see to his right, nor to his left, and also not too far ahead; within the circle of his own thoughts he spins around constantly …and to a great degree.

The second son is handsome, slim, well built; it is enchanting to see him in a fencing pose. He too is clever and furthermore worldly-wise; he has seen plenty, and it seems that even our homeland is more intimately conversant with him than with the stay-at-home. This advantage is certainly neither exclusively nor essentially due to travelling, it belongs rather to the inimitability of this child, acknowledged by anyone who has ever wanted to imitate his multiple somersaults into the water, executed with almost fierce mastery and control. His passion and courage lead to the end of the diving board, but there, the emulator suddenly sits down instead of diving and raises his arms apologetically. Despite all – I should of course be blissfully happy to have such a son – my relationship with him is not unclouded. His left eye is a bit smaller than the right, and he blinks a lot; indeed this is only a small defect that renders his face even more audacious as it would otherwise have been, and no one would attribute the scowling insularity of his character to this blinking eye. I, the father, do so. Of course it is not the physical imperfection that pains me, but a corresponding trivial irregularity in his spirit, some errant poison in the blood, some sort of incompetence that prevents him from fully exploiting his life's potential, which I alone truly appreciate. Then again this makes him indeed my true son, for his imperfection is actually a defect in our whole family, but most salient in this son.

The third son is equally handsome but not in a way that I would value. He has the good looks of a singer: curving mouth; dreamy eyes; head that needs draperies behind it, to make an impact; excessively bulging chest; quick flying hands that drop limp even more easily; legs with insufficient strength to carry his weight. Furthermore: The tone of his voice does not possess enough depth; it deceives momentarily, leaving the connoisseur to listen attentively, but thereupon loses its breath. It is in general alluring to put this son of mine in the limelight; I however prefer to keep him concealed; he himself does not impose, not because he is aware of his limitations, but out of innocence. He also feels something of a stranger in our time; he is often listless, conscious that he belongs to my family but at the same time to another… lost to him forever, from which nothing can enliven him.

The fourth son may be the most affable of all. A true child of his time. He is understood by all, stands on common ground with everyone …for everyone is tempted to give him a nod. Perhaps it is due to this broad appreciation that his essence gains a kind of lightness, his movement a degree of freedom, his judgement a certain insouciance. One would often like to replicate some of his remarks, indeed only some of them, since by and large he suffers from being far too facilitating. He is like one who would fly off admirably, piercing the air like a swallow, but then ending up in the sands of the desert, a non-entity. Such reflections sour my fondness for this child.

The fifth son is benevolent and good-natured; promising less than he has delivered; he is so insignificant that one would literally feel alone in his presence. This has however lent him a degree of reputation. If I were asked how that has come about, I could not offer any answers. Maybe innocence easily permeates the chaotic elements of this world, and innocent he certainly is, perhaps overly innocent. He is friendly to everyone, perhaps overly so. I confess: It does not please me to hear him praised in my presence.

Commending my son, such an obviously admirable person, would indeed cheapen such praise.

My sixth son appears to be the most profound of all, at least at a glance. He is prone to hanging his head down, yet he is an adept orator. It is therefore difficult for one to cope with him. Should he fall into despair, he succumbs to an inconsolable sorrow; should his spirits be high, he maintains it by confident conversation. Indeed, I do not deny that he has a certain tumultuous passion, to which he is oblivious; in the light of the day he battles with his thoughts, as if in a dream. Without being ill – he actually enjoys perfect health – he sometimes staggers, especially in the twilight; he however needs no help and does not fall. Perhaps this phenomenon is caused by his physical development, for he is way too tall for his age. It makes him unsightly as a whole, despite some striking individual traits, for example his beautiful hands and feet. His forehead by the way is also unattractive; and his skin, as well as his bone formation, seems somehow shrunken.

The seventh son belongs to me perhaps more than the others. The world has not valued his worth, for it does not appreciate his particular brand of humour. I do not overvalue him; I know, he is insignificant enough; should it be the world's only misgiving, not to appreciate his worth, it would still remain faultless. I would not wish to be without this son however. He induces a certain turmoil as well as a deference for tradition, combining the two in an unassailable whole, at least this is my impression, but he certainly knows less than anyone how to initiate something with this achievement; he does not set the wheels of the future into motion, but his adeptness is so heartening, so inspiring. I wish he would have children, and these …more children. Alas, it appears this desire will never be fulfilled. With a complacency which I find comprehensible, but equally reprehensible, and which stands in magnificent contradiction to the judgement of his surrounding world, he floats and fumbles around, alone; he does not care about women and will therefore never lose his good disposition.

My eighth son is my child of sorrow and I am actually not aware of any reason for it. He appears like a stranger to me, but I nevertheless feel a fatherly bond with him. Time has healed a great deal but there was occasion when, just thinking about him made me shiver. He goes his own way and has broken off all ties with me; with his hard head and his small athletic body – as a young boy, only his legs were rather frail but that could since have been balanced out – he will certainly break through wherever it pleases him. Occasionally I did feel like recalling him, asking him how he actually was, the reason why he had shut his father out and what he actually intended in life; but he is now so far away and so much time has already gone by, that things should better stay as they are. I hear that he, the only one amongst my sons, has grown a full beard; that is certainly not becoming for a man as small as he is.

My ninth son is very elegant and has what the ladies particularly consider a melting eye. So much so that occasionally, he could even ensnare me; though a wet sponge would be enough to literally wipe away all that unworldly radiance. The peculiarity of this son is that he does not endeavour to be alluring; he would be content to lie down his whole life on the sofa and stare at the ceiling …or still better, let his eyes rest under the eyelids. Were he in this, his preferred state of being, he would then talk, and not idle talk; terse and vivid; but certainly within limits; were he to overstep these boundaries, sometimes inevitable given they are so narrow, his words could become quite empty. One would try to stop him with a wave of the hand, were there any hope his slumberous eyes could notice the gesture.

My tenth son is presumed to have an insincere character. I do not wholly refute nor affirm this shortcoming. Certainly, anyone who sees him approach, in his overly ceremonious tight frock-coat, meticulously cleaned old black hat, a motionless face, the somewhat protruding chin, the heavy bulging eyelids, two fingers often over his lips, anyone who so sees him, would think: 'That he is an absolute hypocrite'. But then...just listen to him speak! Sagacious; thoughtful; brusque; criss-crossing queries with mischievous vitality; in compliance with the entire world in an astonishingly joyful manner. A compliance that inevitably straightens the neck out and uplifts the head. Many a time, through his conversation, he has attracted those who had considered themselves very clever and had been repelled by his appearance. However, there are also people who are indifferent to his looks but find his words hypocritical. I, as a father, will not take any sides here, but I must acknowledge that the latter verdict is note-worthier than the former.

My eleventh son is gentle and probably the weakest amongst my sons; his frailty is however quite deceptive; that is to say he can at times be sturdy and determined, though even then there is somehow an underlying fragility. Yet that is no shameful weakness; it appears so, merely on this earth of ours. For instance, is not eagerness to fly a weakness, given the staggering, uncertainty and flapping involved? My son displays something of that nature. Of course such characteristics in a son do not please a father. They tend to ruin the family. Sometimes he looks at me as if he would wish to tell me: "I will take you with me, Father". Then I think: 'You would be the last person I would trust'. Then again his eyes seem to say: "So let me at least be the last".

These are my eleven sons.

INTERPRETATION

Though Kafka considered himself to be too much of a son to be a father, he writes from a distinctively paternal perspective – indicative of a father's standpoint – about his *Eleven Sons*: Each of these children, so clearly defined and thoughtfully placed, could lead one to see them as reflections of the symbolically significant aspects of his life; for these important facets – instrumental in shaping his character and influencing his development – possess their own distinct features and occupy a unique position in his heart.

The father regards his First Son as superficially unattractive, though he appreciates his steadfast and intelligent nature. This child has an unimpressive narrow viewpoint, making his outlook somewhat limited, from which he is unable to see beyond the small circle of his own thoughts. Did Kafka consider this son to characterise the *Work Persona* he adopted within his day-to-day professional role? Believing this facet of his life to be superficially unappealing, but determined and clever in essence; needing only to operate within fairly narrow limits, resulting in the radius of its thoughts being restricted within specifically defined parameters. Despite this aspect being a necessary part of Kafka, he may well have held little regard for it...as it probably gave him no inspiration.

The Second Son is considered to be attractive, with an impressive physique, wily and graceful, with experience and wisdom at hand, commanding an unusual accord with his homeland that even those who remain at home have not yet acquired. Though the father appreciates this son's characteristics, he is also aware of the imperfections that... to some degree taint ...and, to some degree add ...to his qualities: But it is not the physical imperfections that distress the father, more the irregularity within, which the father acknowledges is inherent in his entire family. Does Kafka consider this son to be a reflection of his *Literary Skill*, appealing at face value as well as in the body of the work, with a graceful demeanour that demonstrates intelligence as well as experience and wisdom, and... with an understanding of his 'homeland' Jewish roots that he may feel even those who are more experienced Zionists do not possess? Though Kafka may appreciate the uniqueness of his *Literary Skill*, he may still have felt it possessed a small flaw which was evident both superficially as well as in its spirit; a reference to the pessimism he felt so greatly, a kind of stray poison running through the lifeblood of his work: Though this pessimism may have affected his entire family – each and every son...or all of the other aspects of his life – it is his *Literary Skill* that reveals illustrates this the most.

The father considers his Third Son to be handsome as well, but holds no regard for this, for the son reacts too quickly... but does not possess the will to maintain his actions; with insufficient strength in his legs, he is unable to support himself adequately; his voice is without the necessary depth, so is unable to maintain itself and hold the attention of those listening; this son has no inclination to be in the spotlight, nor does the father endeavour to put him there... as his naivety leaves him vulnerable; This son appears confused, feeling he belongs not only to his present family, but also to another ...from whom he has been separated forever, and so nothing seems to brighten his mood. Did Kafka consider this son to reflect his *Literature*? Though attractive to him, he holds little regard for it, as he feels it possesses insufficient strength to support itself within the mainstream; he may believe the voice of his work lacks the depth to maintain itself and hold the attention of a wider audience: Therefore, Kafka in not inclined to put his *Literature* in the spotlight, for it embodies an innocence that borders on the naive, making it vulnerable to criticism; this may be why Kafka's work appears confusing, feeling as if it belonged to another literary style that has been lost forever...as well as too its present literary family, which only adds to the ambiguous language within!

The Fourth Son is thought to be the most cordial of all; he appears in complete accord within his present time, genial and agreeable with everyone he encounters ...which only adds to his tranquil demeanour; though one may be tempted to repeat what this son says, such remarks are only few ...and become discredited by his overly accommodating nature; this son appears to promise so much initially, but cannot fulfil these high expectations, resulting in the father's disappointment. Is this son symbolic of Kafka's *Empathy*? with a sincere compassion for the plight of mankind, understood by all it encounters, standings on common ground, and... in complete accord with its time; though others may wish to quote Kafka's empathic dialogue, there is little Kafka feels worthwhile quoting, for the sympathetic nature of his writing undermines its presence in the mainstream. Did Kafka believe his *Empathy* promised so much initially, endeavouring to illustrate humanity's tragic folly, only to lose its essence as time went on, causing him to feel great disappointment?

The father notes the compassion and thoughtfulness of his Fifth Son, who offered more than anyone could expect... but whose presence is somewhat insignificant; though the father confesses he is at a loss for the reputation this son has gained. He is an innocent soul, whose purity the father believes, has allowed him to overcome the chaotic world around, making his innocence all the more evident. The father feels uncomfortable when he hears this son praised, for his reputation is such that any praise loses its value when awarded to him. Is this how Kafka viewed his *Literary Standing* within the literary establishment? Conveying his stories compassionately and portraying his subjects thoughtfully, offering more than anyone could have expected from him, but whose presence is somewhat insignificant; Kafka may admit that he is at a loss for the reputation his *Literary Standing* has achieved, for it is not deliberate in its manner ...but innocent by nature, which is probably the reason why it has not been lost in the literary conventionalism of the day. Kafka may feel uncomfortable to hear his credibility praised, for it probably was not – nor could it ever be – his intention to seek acclaim for his work…which elucidates why he would feel cheapened to be applauded.

The Six Son is the most thoughtful of all, a skilful orator …but susceptible to despair, which makes his mood awkward; during his depressive states he is beyond help or consolation, but when elated, maintains his good mood with reassuring conversation. The father recognises this son's enthusiasm, but notes how he wrestles with his own thoughts …as if in a trance; despite this son's good health he is prone to staggering, especially in the early evening, but he always manages to maintain his balance, unassisted: The father attributes this condition to the son's development… for he is far too tall for his age, with an ugliness in his central features, but an attractiveness in the hands and feet. Did Kafka consider this son to represent his *Creativity*? Thoughtful in approach and skilful in presentation, vulnerable to despair, making its mood somewhat awkward; thus reflected in his literature, for when sombre…it appears beyond hope, though when spirited …it maintains a confident reassurance. Kafka may recognise the enthusiasm his *Creativity* possesses, but appreciates how much it wrestles with its own dilemmas; despite his healthy creative streak, he acknowledges how much it wanes at times, but never sees it falter; maybe it is due to what Kafka believes to be the freakish development of his *Creativity* – an overly advanced nature for its time – that gives the impression of ugliness in its central features but attractiveness in the peripheral aspects of its substance.

Son number Seven belongs to his father the most, though he is not overly valued by him; for the father believes the world does not appreciate his son's humour; despite this, he still considers this son to be faultless. The father recognises the disorder, as well as the appreciation for tradition, this son brings, combining these two qualities to achieve something significant; it is for this very reason that the father notes he would not like to be without his seventh son. Though he believes this son will not be responsible for

79

dictating future events, the father does however recognise that he holds a significant skill and understanding that is greatly reassuring; he wishes this child to have children of his own, but realises he will never fulfil this wish due to his self-satisfied nature, which leaves him without desire for female company; this will in itself... ensure he would always maintain his precious way of being. Does Kafka consider this son to be the embodiment of his *Truth*? This *Truth*, belonging to him more than any other facet of his life, which he does not overrate, for he believes the world around to be incapable of appreciating its unique sense of humour. Kafka recognises the chaos his *Truth* brings, along with its value for tradition...which it combines to achieve what he considers to be something important, and why he considers the *Truth* of his work to be faultless. Kafka may imply he would never like to live without his *Truth* at the heart of his work, even though he might feel that it would not influence the future of literature – of course he did not know at the time just how much of an influence it would have – he finds great reassurance in its skill and understanding. Though Kafka may want his *Truth* to be passed down through the generations, he may also recognise that with so little of his work published, his *Truth* would never get the chance to pass down the seeds of its ideology.

The Eighth Son is a dejected soul who has become a stranger to his father; though he does not know why the son has turned out this way, he still feels his strong paternal connection. Much time has passed and there has been some healing of old wounds, but this son has chosen to break off all communication. The father notes the son's athletic build and hard-headedness... appreciating the tenacious nature of this child will overcome whatever he puts his mind to; he has considered contacting him and trying to reconcile their strained relationship – with a perplexing curiosity as to why this son has reacted the way he has – but all appears to have gone too far to rekindle any spark of a connection. The

Eighth Son is the only one of the children to have grown a beard, which the father remarks, would not befit a person with his diminutive stature. Is the Eighth Son a reflection of Kafka's relationship with his father Hermann? A forlorn connection which has become something of a stranger to him; though he does not fully understand why this relationship has turned sour, Kafka may still feel a strong kinship. The passage of time could have healed much of the hurt Kafka felt, but the connection with his father appears to have broken down …permanently; he may reminisce about the strength and tenacity this relationship once held, as it determinedly proceeded through all circumstances both good and bad. Though Kafka may wish to dwell on this relationship, he now concedes this would be of no benefit, for it has moved on, and so should he. Perhaps the beard the son now sports is symbolic of how disguised their relationship now appears …almost beyond recognition.

The father speaks of his Ninth Son as an elegant individual with an alluring eye for the ladies, and an attraction so engaging that on occasion even he could be captivated; however, this superficial magnificence could easily be wiped away with only a wet sponge: The father sees that this son is unintentionally alluring, as he appears to be more content to sit back and rest; when at ease, the son engages in conversation, short and potent; but his subject matter is undoubtedly limited, for should he overstep his boundaries his words would lose their meaning… though he is too preoccupied with his own conversation to be stopped in mid-flow. Does Kafka believe this son to be an illustration of his *Innocence*? With a certain style that appeals to those of a gentler persuasion, as even the great man himself admits to being captivated by; despite the superficial appeal of his *Innocence*, Kafka believes that it would take nothing more than a damp cloth to wipe away its earthly brilliance. Though this facet could be somewhat peculiar and unintentionally alluring, Kafka may have felt it was most content when at rest, as this limited its exposure to the turbulent stirrings of his writing; when feeling at ease …this *Innocence* feels free to speak to Kafka – in brief but none-the-less influential tones, though it is restricted in its knowledge and can lose its strength of purpose if it steps beyond its narrow margins of understanding. Kafka may concede that this *Innocence* of his can become so pre-occupied with its conversation that he finds it difficult to interrupt it in mid-flow.

The father notes that others consider his Tenth Son to be disingenuous, but he is unable to acknowledge this; he recognises the son's appearance provokes this belief, for his style of dress and mannerism suggest that he is may not be genuine. Then he speaks, with a depth of conversation, intelligence and foresight coupled with challenging and playful tones, in accord with the world around. The father identifies two distinct parties who see the son in opposing lights: The first are taken in by the son's conversation, as they too feel clever and are drawn to his banter, yet find his appearance unappealing; the second party is uninterested in this son's appearance but finds his conversation sanctimonious. The father claims that he will not wholly agree with either opinion, but is inclined to acknowledge the latter. Is the Tenth Son symbolic of Kafka's *Objectivity*? With its appearance and mannerism considered insincere, though Kafka is unable to confirm or deny this. However, it is only when Kafka's literary work speaks to its audience that it demonstrates a depth of understanding, of wisdom and insightfulness, cleverly interlaced with an inquisitive and… at times… almost playful nature, with all these characteristics existing in harmony with the world around. Kafka recognises the distinct groups who view his work; those who consider themselves intelligent, academically astute and worldly wise, becoming attracted to its content, but find its presentation unappealing…with an unconventional style and confusing language; the other group holds a different view, with no interest in his work or its appearance, for they do not appreciate his literary offerings and find its meaning hypocritical.

The father thinks of the Eleventh Son as a tender child and the most fragile of them all, though his delicate disposition can be misleading; despite his obvious frailty, this son can on occasion demonstrate a strong and resolute character. The father remarks that this son's disposition is nothing to be ashamed of, nonetheless, such a trait is not something to please him; for this weakness is a characteristic which can destroy a family. He recognises the look in the son's eyes which suggests he will take the father with him, but he trusts this son the least. Did Kafka consider this son to represent his *Health*? A fragile facet of his life which is by its nature gentle in essence, but surprisingly strong and resolute on occasion. Though Kafka confesses he feels no shame for his frail *Health*, it is nevertheless a feature of his life that does not please him; for it may contribute to the difficulties in his family ...or more relevantly his literary kinship. Kafka may compare the inviting trust of the eleventh son to the heartfelt feeling he gets from his Health, where it asks him to entrust himself to it; unfortunately for Kafka... it was the very last thing he must entrust himself to!

Eleven Sons is as relevant to Kafka's life as it is to everybody's life. If one considers the influential facets of a man's life to be his sons – just as a woman's are her daughters – then these children, born within the paternity of our existence, appearing and developing at different stages of our lives, each with a unique personality of their own, hold a distinctive position. As we raise these children, we influence their growth as they influence ours!

UNMASKING OF A CONFIDENCE TRICKSTER

Finally, around ten o'clock, I arrived in front of the grand house where I had been invited for the evening's entertainment, with a man whom until now I barely knew, who had unexpectedly thrust himself upon me, again, and had me wandering about the streets for two hours.

'Well!' I said, and clapped my hands as a sign of the absolute urgency in saying goodbye. I had certainly tried the same, less noticeably, a few times before, and was already exhausted.

"Are you going straight in?" he asked. I heard a noise in his mouth similar to the clashing of teeth.

'Yes', I replied.

I was indeed invited, I had already told him; but the invitation was to go inside, where I longed to be, and not standing here, outside the doors, staring beyond the ears of this stranger; now here I am keeping his company, both of us trapped in this moment of silence, as if we had chosen to wait and allow time to pass on this spot.

Yet the houses all around us and the darkness above reaching up to the stars also took part in this silence; and the footsteps of indiscernible pedestrians whose paths one had no desire to guess, the wind blowing with such force – against the other side of the street, a gramophone singing melodies behind the closed windows of some room, these too listened to the silence as if it were theirs, since the beginning of time and for ever after.

And my companion – having given a smile – yielded to it in his name as well as mine, extended his right arm up along the wall and leaned his face against it, his eyes closed. I did not follow that smile quite to the end, for shame overwhelmed me. It was only when seeing that smile and nothing else, that I first recognised him as a confidence trickster. Yet I had been in this city for months on end and had believed to have known all about confidence tricksters, how they deliberately appeared out of the side streets at night to confront us, hands stretched out like innkeepers; how they hung about the poster-boards next to where we stand, as if playing hide and seek, spying with at least one eye from behind these placards; how they suddenly appear and hover around us at intersections when we are anxious and afraid on the edge of the pavement! I understood them so well, they were indeed my first acquaintances in the town's smaller public houses, and it is to them that I owed my first feelings of intransigence within the world, now unimaginable without it, and which I have already begun to feel even inside myself. How they stood abreast, even when we had long since run free …and when there was no one to entrap! Amazing how they did not sit, did not fall; they rather stared at us trying to be convincing…even from afar!

And their means were always the same: They placed themselves before us, as broadly as they could; tried to deter us from whatever we were aspiring to; they provided a haven within the comfort of their bosom, and when at last our feelings gathered and rose up against them, they took it as an embrace into which they threw themselves, face first.

And I have recognised these old peculiarities for the first time, having endured this man's company for far too long. I rubbed my fingertips together in order to undo the disgrace.

My uninvited companion was still standing as before, fancying himself even more as a confidence trickster, and blushing with satisfaction over his destiny.

'Exposed!' said I, and tapped him gently on the shoulder. I then hurried up the stairs and the disinterested – though reassuring – faces of the staff in the hallway delighted me, like an exquisite surprise. I looked at them all in succession while they took my coat and dusted my boots clean. Taking a deep breath and standing tall, I then entered the living room.

INTERPRETATION

Though we may see a person's face a thousand times, we will never truly see what lies within their heart. Many strive to live decent lives, fostering a virtuous code of goodwill and honest toil; but these good natured souls can so easily fall into the clutches of others who choose to live by a different code: These ruthless opportunists seek the trust of the kind-hearted and vulnerable, the lonely and isolated, using their seductive charms to offer false friendship: These are life's confidence tricksters. These con artists aim to win the trust of others, in the hope of taking their treasures: So when confronted by such deceptive characters, vigilance is the armour of protection one will need to stave off potential heartache. Kafka's *Unmasking a Confidence Trickster* is a cautionary tale that stirs the imagination... as well as stoking the fires of awareness.

The narrator finally arrives at the grand house where he has been invited for the evening, having endured the company of an uninvited stranger who forces himself upon him. Does Kafka exclaim his relief at finally arriving before his literary desk, where his creativity invited him to spend the evening, after having to tolerate the company of his own confidence trickster? Kafka's trickster may be his own insecurity, his doubts and fears that could so easily undermine his self-belief, unsettling him and disrupting his literary flow.

Though more subtle attempts have been made by the narrator to rid himself of his unwanted guest, there appears to be no easy escape, as the persistence of this charlatan is steadfast ...prolonging his companionship. For Kafka, – as for so many – the unrelenting determination of these tricksters is exhausting, as they press ahead with their devious ruse. Upon the narrator's arrival at the house, the trickster finds himself on the cusp of seeing all his endeavours thwarted, and so he falls silent, in a final attempt to capture his victim whilst contemplating the next move. It is this time of silence that provides the greatest clarity for the narrator, for it gives him the opportunity to settle his thoughts, whilst the trickster is forced into more desperate measures. Does Kafka reveal how he allows himself to be tormented by his trickster up until the very end, to the point where he reaches his destination, pausing momentarily to take in the silence, and there, within his composed mind finds the necessary clarity of thought? This quiet moment, where one's mind finds insight, when one's thoughts become clear, is vital to allow the whirlpool of emotion and irrationality to dissolve ...and so allow transparency; whilst this very same moment will expose those devious characters, as they inadvertently reveal themselves through their actions.

When the narrator recognises that he has allowed himself to endure the company of the stranger for too long a time, without his experience alerting him that his companion was a trickster all along, he is consumed by shame. Is Kafka ashamed for not recognising his tricksters sooner, when experience abandons him, and out of courtesy or ignorance... he fails to identify when he is being deceived? Kafka sees how these tricksters appear from the side streets of his mind, these unscrupulous doubts that step out to make their presence known, reaching out with welcoming arms, as he strolls along the avenues of his creativity; these insecurities who loiter around his thoughts, playing a game of hide-and-seek with his creative confidence ...whilst maintaining at least one watchful eye on his every move; how these deceptive tricksters stay close to Kafka's side when he is uncertain and anxious of how to proceed, as he waits at the intersection of his thoughts, hovering on the edge. Kafka appears to know these confidence tricksters so well, and is astonished by their persistence; for regardless of their failure, of the scorn and rejection they endure, they never admit defeat, never relinquish an opportunity, take up their position as boldly as possible... welcoming him into their empty hearts like a cherished friend. What else is Kafka left to do now, but expose his trickster and escape its clutches, then venture forth and enter his literary house for his creative evening ahead!

The essence of *Unmasking a Confidence Trickster* illustrates the need to be cautious of those who try too much to win another person's trust: For these may all too often have a dubious agenda. Though others may try to win, buy or demand someone's trust, or even their love, respect, admiration or friendship, these should instead be earned through a timely demonstration of genuine and purposeful actions. Confidence tricksters exist in many guises, so continual vigilance is vital: They range from those individuals who wish to deceive us for personal gain, through to businesses who use clever advertising to prey on people's weaknesses and win their custom. So when these creatures of deceit appear before us, ready to devour our trust and feast on our good will, it will be necessary to demonstrate the strength of character to liberate ourselves from undesirable company ...without hesitation or reluctance.

A CROSSBREED

I have a most unusual animal, half kitten, and half lamb. It is an inheritance from my father; it has however developed... whilst in my possession; before, it was much more of a lamb than a kitten, and now possesses both characteristics equally. From the cat it has the head and the claws, from the lamb the size and the shape; from both, its eyes, flickering and meek; the fur is short and soft; as for movements, it leaps as well as crawls; in the sunshine it curls up in a ball on the windowsill and purrs; it runs about in the meadows, so fast no one can catch up with it; it flees from cats, attacks lambs; in the moonlight its preferred walk-way is up in the guttering; it cannot mew and loathes rats; it can lie still and wait for hours... on the prowl, next to the chicken-coop, but has indeed never seized the opportunity for murder. I feed it with milk that it appears to prefer best, which it sucks in through its predatory fangs. Naturally it is a great spectacle for children.

Sunday afternoon is the visiting time, I put the little beast on my lap and the children from the entire neighbourhood gather around me. They ask the most peculiar questions that no human being can answer: Why is there only one such animal? Why do I, rather than anyone else... own it? Has there ever been a similar animal before? What would happen if it died? Does it feel lonely? Why doesn't it have any offspring? What is its name? ...and the like. I do not make any effort to answer, I am rather content just to show off what I own, without further explanation. Sometimes the children bring cats along; once, they even brought two lambs. However, contrary to their expectations, there was not a spark of recognition, the animals merely looked at each other calmly, out of animal eyes, and evidently... mutually accepted their entity as a divine fact.

On my lap, the animal does not feel any fear or inclination for a chase. It feels most comfortable clung to me. It remains faithful to the family that has brought it up. This is certainly not out of some kind of exceptional loyalty, rather the real instinct of an animal that has innumerable step-relatives on this earth, but perhaps not even one blood relation; it therefore treasures as sacred, the protection it has found with us. Sometimes I laugh when it sniffs around me and wriggles through my legs; it will not part from me. It is not enough for it to be a kitten and a lamb, it almost wants to be a dog as well. Once, when I was overburdened with my business affairs – just as might happen to anybody – and I could not find a way out, I felt like forfeiting everything, and while reclining in a rocking chair, with the little beast on my lap, I casually looked down and saw tears falling from its gigantic whiskers. Were they mine, or the creatures? Did this cat, along with the soul of a sheep, have also a man's ambition? I have inherited so little from my father, but this one is certainly remarkable.

I believe the turmoil the beast feels stems from within both the cat and the lamb, as diverse as they are… its skin is too tight for it. Sometimes, it jumps up on the chair next to me, braces itself against my shoulder and holds its snout to my ear. It looks as if it wants to tell me something, in fact it bends forward and stares me in the face to observe the impression the message had left. To appease it, I pretend as if I had understood its intention and nod. It then jumps down on the floor and dances around. Perhaps the butcher's knife would be a salvation for this creature, something which I shall withhold from it, since the beast is a legacy from my father. It should therefore wait until its last breath leaves of its own accord on its own, even if there are times when it looks at me with discerning human eyes that invite me to do that very thing!

INTERPRETATION

Kafka's crossbreed is indeed a most curious beast, a thoroughly unique entity, possessing the characteristics of two very different animals, an undoubtedly peculiar legacy for any father to pass down to his son: Such a bizarre creation makes one wonder what it was that inspired Kafka to envisage – and so thoughtfully write about – this fascinating creature? Did Kafka consider the hybrid animal to be a reflection of the two main influences in his life... namely his professional duty and his literary role? The feline nature of the creature possesses the predatory instincts of a hunter, a fighter and a killer, reflecting the literary beast within Kafka, hunting down his literary themes, fighting the oppression of conventionalism, and killing the tedium of mediocrity. The ovine influence side of the beast illustrates Kafka's day-to-day profession, in which he finds himself casually grazing on the mundane matters of course ...in a somewhat docile state; could this provide an insightful glimpse into the mindset of one of literature's most enigmatic and thought-provoking writers?

The narrator admits he has an unusual animal, inherited from his father, but developing during his lifetime; though the lamb's side of the creature was initially more dominant, the crossbreed now possesses characteristics of both lamb and kitten equally. Are these Kafka's thoughts on the development of his own character, a legacy passed down from his father... but flourishing within his lifetime, starting off as more of a lawyer than a writer – more lamb than kitten – but now containing both facets equally, and bound together within an unusual single entity ...Kafka himself? The head and claws of the crossbreed are taken from the cat, reflecting the creative nature of Kafka ...with his sharp feline features, through which his literary instincts taste, hear and smell life's rich experience; the claws of the cat are the talons with which Kafka seizes his subjects, firmly sinking his nails into the themes he gets to grips with. The size and shape of the crossbreed are taken from the lamb, implying Kafka's full and solid presence, a necessary characteristic within his professional role. The eyes are shared by both lamb and kitten, or in Kafka's case ...both lawyer and writer – objective and subjective – viewing life from two very different sides so as to provide a well-rounded perspective. The crossbreed is completely at ease either playing like a lamb or prowling around like a cat, though its preferred nourishment is milk, which it takes in through its feline fangs. Here Kafka reveals his contentment in either professional or literary role; within his legal duties he rushes about scarcely to be caught, after which, he curls up on his literary window-sill ...basking in the contentment of his work, eagerly awaiting the evening where he will once again prowl around his literary desk ...ready to stalk the subjects for his stories; it appears the sustenance for the creature is more suited to the kitten than the lamb, suggesting that the source of nourishment that best suited Kafka best was that which fuelled his creative needs.

The creature is a fascinating spectacle for children, who visit the narrator and his faithful companion every Sunday. These gatherings inspire great intrigue in so many, who frequently question the narrator who in turn chooses not to respond, as he feels unable to provide the answers that would satisfy these curious young minds. Is this an insight into how Kafka viewed his work, believing that those who ask too many questions about his own hybrid creature appear to be nothing more than curious children asking questions he feels no need to answer? For Kafka, such question-bearers may appear to be trapped within the confines of conventional thinking, unable to appreciate his literature for what it is, without over analysing or intellectualising its meaning. Are the children's questions essentially the same Kafka asks himself, thus provoking a candid admission of his own uncertainty in finding answers? He may have chosen not to respond simply because he did not know, which elucidates why he claimed he didn't want his work interpreted! Though the Sunday afternoon visitors bring along other cats and sheep to see the creature's reaction ...it feels no malice toward them. This illustrates Kafka's complete accord in the company of other lawyers and writers, feeling no need for competition, no threat from their presence, just recognition of their similarities.

The crossbreed is most content when at rest on the narrator's lap, feeling no fear nor need for escape: Both sheep and kitten are in perfect harmony with their master when situated close to him, just as both professional and creative sides of Kafka may have existed in perfect accord ...when held close to his heart. The instinctive faithfulness of the creature to the narrator's family may imply that Kafka maintained his instinctive faithfulness to his family; though many of his relations possessed similar traits as himself, not one shared exactly the same blend of his unique personality; perhaps the narrator's remark about the crossbreed not being content as a cat or a lamb... but instead almost wanting to be a dog, could be Kafka's belief that his own crossbred influences possess something of a canine loyalty. The narrator speaks of the time whilst troubled in his business affairs, when he saw tears falling from the gigantic whiskers of the crossbreed as it sat on his lap, unsure whether these belonged to the creature or himself, and uncertain of whether the crossbreed possessed not only its own characteristics but also some of his. Does Kafka reveal that when he is troubled by difficulties in his affairs the main aspects of his character become unsettled as well? Because his crossbreed follows him so devotedly through life, sharing each experience along his journey, such empathic feelings are certain to be shared with its master. The narrator claims he has inherited little from his father, but the legacy of the crossbreed is indeed a remarkable one: Is this an admission by Kafka that he has inherited little from his father, though the legacy that influences his life so powerfully... is a truly remarkable one?!

The narrator attributes the restlessness of the crossbreed to both characteristics of the animal, which in turn causes its skin to be too tight. Does Kafka attribute his restlessness to the main influences in his life, as they struggle for dominance… almost appearing to be two distinctly different animals forced to live within a single body, making him feel confined inside his own skin? The crossbreed occasionally jumps up beside the narrator, pressing its snout against his ear as if it had something to share, then looking at him to see his reaction: Did Kafka believe his crossbred influences sought his attention, pressing themselves so intimately on his consciousness whilst pretending to pass on a message, but all the time merely looking for the much needed assurance of their importance in his life? Though the narrator had contemplated ending the creature's life at the hands of the butcher, he eventually decides to spare it this indignity, allowing it to live out its natural course, despite the crossbreed looking at him occasionally as if to imply this is what it wants most. Perhaps Kafka now exposes the true extent of his turmoil and frustration, the deep despair that may have compelled him on so many occasions to want to put an end to both his legal and literary careers …or ultimately, to do away with himself!

Is Kafka's crossbreed only a fictional beast… an invention of his imaginative creativity, or could we all possess a crossbreed of our own? Do we have a loyal creature that is uniquely ours, inherited from our forefathers but developing in our time, a creature that comprises different animalistic origins reflecting the main influences of our personality, a beast we feed and care for, that is devoted only to us, sharing our joys and sorrows, but at the same time… possessing troubles of its own, and all confined within a single entity …Ourselves!

THE CITY COAT OF ARMS

In the beginning, the construction of the Tower of Babel went along in tolerable order; the order was indeed too ideal, one thought perhaps too much about guides, interpreters, workers' accommodation and lines of communication, as if there laid ahead the possibility of centuries to undertake this work. Actually, the then ruling opinion was that one could not build slowly enough; but of course this could not be exaggerated and one could not at all recoil from laying the foundations. Thus was made the argument:

The essential part of the whole enterprise is the decision to build a tower which reaches into the heavens. All else is secondary next to this pursuit. The idea, once conceived in such splendour, cannot vanish; so long as there are humans around, there will also exist the powerful yearning to complete the tower. Therefore, one should have no anxiety with regard to the future; on the contrary, man's knowledge continually develops, and will progress even further; a work for which we would need one year today, could perhaps be completed in half a year within a hundred years; furthermore, it would be better and more durable. So why toil away to the extreme of one's powers? It would have only made sense if one could hope to complete the tower in one generation's time, something which is of course beyond all anticipation. It is more likely that the next generation, with its perfected knowledge, will find the work of the previous generation inadequate and will thus tear down the old constructions, in order to start anew. Such thoughts crippled the ruling forces, and rather than worrying about the tower, they concentrated on the construction of the workers' city. Every ethnicity sought the most beautiful quarter for itself, and this led to many disputes and eventually bloody conflicts. The battles came to no end; to the leaders this proved to be new evidence that – given the lack of necessary focus – the construction of the tower should be done very slowly, and preferably after a universal peace accord had been reached. Indeed, time was not spent exclusively on battles; during the recesses the cities were embellished, something that provoked new jealousy and new conflicts. Thus the age of the first generation went by, but none of the following ones proved any different; of course the craftsmanship developed, and with that the number of conflicts. Moreover, the second and third generations recognised the mindlessness of building a heaven-ascending tower; and by that time, people were way too involved with each other to want to leave the city.

All that has emerged in this city from its legends and songs, is imbued with the yearning for a prophesied day, when the city would be smashed by a giant fist in five consecutive blows. This is the reason a fist appears on the city coat of arms.

INTERPRETATION

Every generation occupies a unique position in the course of time, a creation of its predecessors, and the creator of its successors, existing in a period that is beyond what has passed …and never to be lived through again: Each generation holds the key to how the advancements of the past were sculpted, so as to shape the world for the future; all generations aspire to leave their own legacy, achievements that serve as a mark of their contribution, a distinctive reminder to their successors that the world they occupy will be better for what has been left for them. *The City Coat of Arms* illustrates how the aspirations of any generation need to be implemented practically – even if only the first building blocks – else they could be lost altogether, as those who follow on may not share the same energy or spirit to continue.

The Tower of Babel is a biblical story taken from The Book of Genesis, about a united humanity that migrates from the East to inhabit the city of Babel, the Hebrew name for Babylon: These people, speaking only one language, envisioned a tower of such magnificence that it would reach into the heavens, though not in the honour of God, but in dedication to their own skill ...as a monument to Man's greatness. Since it had been God's intention for Man to procreate and spread across the Earth, he intervened, confusing the language so as to divide the people and force them to scatter across the Earth.

Kafka's adaptation of this biblical story illustrates the short-sightedness of the first generation of settlers in Babel, as they strived for absolute perfection whilst planning the construction of their monumental tower: Their idealism along with their anticipation of future generations being more technologically advanced, resulted in their energy and spirit draining away. The assumption that the successive generations would develop better skills and greater technology paralysed the initial settlers; they focused solely on perfecting their plans before commencing construction... with catastrophic consequences. Although scrupulous planning was vital for this prodigious project, it was none-the-less critical for construction to begin on the tower: Kafka suggests that the first generation's inaction was inconsequential, for Man's eternal ambition to build such monuments in his own honour ensures that the tower's construction would be too great an achievement to resist. However, could the first generation feel assured that their monumental tower would be built by their successors, or would their successors choose instead to build a monument to themselves? Therefore, what would be initial settlers' legacy to the world?

As procrastination sets in, division and disharmony take hold, and the unified humanity that had come to Babel with a common cause, is now steeped in jealousy and rivalry, which leads them to conflict and bloodshed. The need to get underway with constructing the tower was great, for it would have maintained unity and focus, as all would be working toward the ultimate goal. The problems that can arise when one focuses solely on perfection, without balancing it out with practical application, soon become all too evident. The longer the delay in getting the project underway, the deeper the rift between the nationalities …leading to greater conflicts, and – just as the story relays – the initial purpose is eventually lost as the quest for power amongst the races becomes their only purpose. The more time passes, the more settled the separate nationalities become, building specific infrastructures for themselves and competing for dominance. Ironically, the first generation planned to build a tower to reach the heavens, but their inaction resulted in the successive generations creating a city more akin to hell. What could have been a city with a monument to Man's greatness, descended into a divided city which became a monument to Man's inaction. The later generations recognised the senselessness of building the great tower, realising the disputes amongst all sides would make it impossible to undertake the project in harmony: Since they had settled and established their own communities, they now had to tolerate these circumstances, as none chose to seek peace …nor leave. Ironically, had Man elected to build this tower in honour of God, there would be no disharmony, no division, no petty squabbles descending into bloody conflicts, just an absolute necessity to complete a monument to the mysterious Almighty who lives on in his heart and mind; however, since Man planned to build this monument in his own honour, he exposed his lust for power, his need to reign supreme, and his willingness to spill blood; thus The Tower, this incredible monument reaching into the Heavens, in honour of Man's unity and great skill …became the crumbling ruins of his shameful lust for glory!

The story speaks of the legends and songs yearning for the prophesised day when five successive blows from a giant fist destroy the city of Babel; which is why the coat of arms has a closed fist on it. Perhaps Kafka suggests that Man can create either heaven or hell, right here on Earth: Mankind can build monuments that show his skill and aptitude to achieve greatness, allowing him to border on the divine, or, through his selfish greed and lust for power, Man can destroy the opportunity to prove his worth and justify his existence: If he chooses the former... his generation will live on through history, if he chooses the latter ...the ledgers of history may not record that he even existed.

Is it possible that Kafka used *The City Coat of Arms* to illustrate the folly of Mankind when he attempts to build great monuments in his own honour, instead of maintaining the unity he enjoys in the name of religion? When Man forms large societies, developing monumental systems such as politics and law, striving to create perfection and make them divine, then his selfish ego and lust for power dooms him to failure and conflict. Or, did Kafka consider the legend of the Tower of Babel to reflect his life's work? The short-sightedness of the first generation – who planned so meticulously but did not act – may symbolise Kafka's literature, with so much written ...but so little published! Could this troubled author have believed that the successive generations of writers would possess greater skill, thus making his work appear less important? Or did Kafka consider the Tower of Babel, designed to be a monument reaching the heavens, to be his own literary tower, planned in honour of himself... so he could ascend into the Divine? The united humanity speaking only one language, settling in Babel, could embody Kafka's writing skills; with only one purpose, that of unifying his literature for a greater cause. The intervention of God, who confused the languages and scattered the nationalities, may reflect Kafka's creativity; intervening so as to diversify his literary themes. This may explain why Kafka's language can appear confusing, with his subject matter seeming somewhat scattered. Ironically, with Kafka's illness taking his life so prematurely, and with him publishing so little, he never saw the tower he meticulously planned for ...ascending into the literary heavens!

So what intriguing lesson could be taken from *The City Coat of Arms*? Maybe it is the need to strike a balance between striving for perfection and applying oneself practically. A plan without action is nothing more than a thought... and what purpose would this serve? Though it can also be counter-productive to undertake anything important without careful planning first. If we want to create something significant, and wish for those who come after us to continue our work, we must make a start, so this will act, at the very least, as a guide to follow. If we choose not to contribute because we feel what we offer is not significant, we fail not only ourselves, but our successors too, for it is crucial to recognise and cherish our own contribution. If we wish to build a monument to the heavens, then it is up to us to provide at least the first few steps that lead the way ...for those who will follow on.

THE CITY COAT OF ARMS

A Tower built to reach the heavens, a monument to Man
In pursuit of pure perfection, without construction... just a plan

Migrating mankind came united, from the East all had arrived
One language was their mother tongue... with careful thought
contrived

To demonstrate their brilliance...they'd build this Tower to the
sky
A shrine to praise humanity... for them to worship from up
high

Aspiring for the ultimate... with every detail kept in mind
With nothing left to doubt or chance... so Man could revel in
his Kind

But far too long was spent considering... every brick and its
right place
Wasting time and hope and energy... which they could not
replace

Delayed for days and weeks then months and years... and even
longer still
The initial point that brought them here... no longer had its
will

Trapped by idealism... gone are unified decisions
Now selfishness and glory's needs... are the roots of their
division

So there may be a message... to the worthy and the wise
Not only plan, but build and make your mark... for surely this
implies

The legacy that we leave behind, for generations... without
instruction
Means The City Coat of Arms... will bring inevitable
destruction!

PROMETHEUS

Four legends pertain to Prometheus:

According to the first, he was bound to a rock in the Caucasus, for he had betrayed the Gods... in favour of Mankind; as punishment, the Gods sent great eagles to devour his ever-growing liver.

According to the second legend, Prometheus, anguished by the pain of the ripping beaks, pressed himself ever further into the rock until he became one with it.

According to the third, his betrayal was forgotten over a thousand years, the Gods forgot, the eagles forgot ...and even Prometheus himself.

According to the fourth legend, everyone tired of the mindless affair, the gods tired and the eagles tired of it, the wound closed in tiresomely.

There remained the inexplicable rock. The legend seeks to explain the unexplained. It hails from an undercurrent of truth, it must therefore end in the inexplicable!

INTERPRETATION

The confinement and torture of Prometheus present yet another peculiar subject as part of Kafka's creative bounty: This short parable leaves one to contemplate why the predicament of Greek mythology's creator of Mankind is so alluring to this author; perhaps it is the legendary endeavours of this great character, coupled with his torture... that held such significance for Kafka!

Prometheus, whose name means 'forethought', possessed the ability to see into the future: He was entrusted with the task of creating mankind... whom he moulded from clay, and became a champion of his creation, but this devotion to mankind brought him into conflict with Zeus, the king of the gods. Prometheus enraged Zeus by firstly tricking the gods out of the best portion of the sacrificial feast, giving the meat to man and the bones to them; he then stole fire from heaven and delivered it to mankind, hidden in a fennel stalk. Zeus was so enraged he ordered Prometheus to be chained to a rock in the Caucasus, and had eagles devour his mortal liver each day, only for it to grow back every night. Having endured this punishment over a lengthy period, Prometheus was released from his bonds by the hero Herakles, who killed the eagles before setting him free.

Kafka refers to four legends concerning Prometheus: His punishment as a consequence of betrayal, his endurance of pain and suffering, the memory of his treachery fading over time, and the tiresome nature of his repetitive punishment. Franz Kafka had a severely strained relationship with his father Hermann, whom he considered to have been profoundly 'emotionally abusive' towards him …as outlined in his highly noted *Letter to his Father*. It is therefore possible, that Kafka considered his life to possess similarities to the plight of Prometheus; with his father Hermann exhibiting the same dominating presence as that of Zeus, inflicting what Franz may have believed to be a similar punishment to that of Prometheus; the eagles who attacked Prometheus may be symbolic of the guilt Hermann instils in his son, tearing at him everyday …devouring something vital inside: The four legends thus illustrate the legacy of suffering Franz felt he had endured.

The first legend refers to Prometheus being bound to a rock in the Caucasus after betraying the gods, and eagles sent everyday to devour his liver… which was perpetually renewed. This legend may reflect the stern and uncompromising attitude of Franz's father towards him; were Hermann's feelings of disappointment and betrayal – due to his son's choices – became so very evident? As a result, Franz believes himself to be bound to his own metaphorical rock, this being the obligation to satisfy his father's wishes. Hermann may have used the most powerful weapon at his disposal… Guilt, to attack Franz on a daily basis, destroying something crucial within his son regularly, and for some time to come, only for this vital component to consistently grow back when Franz found comfort in his writing. Prometheus enraged Zeus by caring too much for his creation …mankind, just as Kafka may have enraged his father by caring too much for his literature… instrumental in highlighting the plight of mankind.

The second legend states that due to the torment of the eagle's beaks ripping at his flesh, Prometheus pressed himself further into the rock until both he and the rock became one. Kafka may have decided that the only way to relieve the pain and pressure of the guilt tearing away at him was to press himself deeper into his own rock …his literature: For the more he pressed himself into his literary work …the more he became one with it, and so found salvation from the turmoil of his punishment.

The third legend recalls the treachery of Prometheus being forgotten by all concerned, and over the course of a thousand years, the gods and eagles forgot, as well as Prometheus himself. Does this imply that with the passing of time, the feelings of betrayal and disappointment Hermann may have felt were forgotten, the pressure of the guilt receded, and even Franz forgot… as the memories that were once so painful for him slowly faded over time?

The fourth legend speaks of all involved growing tired of this unnecessary affair; for the gods and eagles tired of it, even the wound healed wearily. This may symbolise Hermann growing weary of his overbearing attitude towards Franz; surely Hermann must have come to accept his son's choices over time: The acceptance by the father of the path chosen by his son, and one he could not influence nor alter; though Franz may have tried to appease his father initially, he did not relent, but remained true to himself.

107

The parable concludes by highlighting the incomprehensible rock: Though the story endeavours to clarify the inexplicable, it rises from an undercurrent of truth, so must remain unexplainable. Could this 'inexplicable rock' represent Kafka's literature? This solid and constant ideal which Kafka was bound to, causing the tearing beaks of guilt imposed by his father to attack him for such a lengthy time, and all because he cared too much for the plight of his creation ...his 'inexplicable' literature! imposed commitments to which he felt bound by his father? Franz was bound to this rock of obligation, and thereafter, continually savaged by the tearing beaks of guilt, all because he cared too much for the plight of his own literary creations! The undercurrent of truth must surely refer to Kafka's truth, the truth as he sees it, not necessarily the truth as it appears to others, but reality as Kafka conceives... his own 'inexplicable' reality!

Though parallels can be drawn between the plight of Prometheus and Kafka's life, comparisons can also be drawn from the lives of so many. The guilt projected by those who exert influence over our lives, can all too often bind us to undesirable obligations. This guilt can be used as a means of control, and is born out of the disappointment others feel when we do not live up to their expectations. Though our parents, partners, friends and peers may want us to follow their example or instruction, is it right to make us slaves of obligation... using the cruel hand of guilt to force us into submission? Such obligations may sometimes be necessary or occasionally beneficial, they might even make us better people, but ultimately the associated guilt becomes a vicious beast that rips away at our happiness and contentment; the lasting scars this may leave will only serve to remind us that we have become a servant to another person's disappointment, because we didn't show compassion for the plight of our own unique creation ...Ourselves!

FIRST SORROW

A trapeze artist – whose art, practiced high in the domes of the great Variety theatres, is known as one of the most difficult human beings can accomplish – had organised his life in such a way, that as long as he worked in the same company... he remained on the trapeze by day and by night; this was at first due to his endeavours for perfection, but it later became a tyrannical custom. All his needs, very unpretentious at that, were met by attendants who took turns and kept watch from way down below, and sent up whatever he required in a specially constructed container – pulling down that which he no longer wanted. This lifestyle created no particular inconvenience for the theatrical troop, except during the turns of the other acts; as he remained unhidden aloft, albeit always quiet during those performances, every so often a stray glance from the public found its way towards him, which was a little disturbing. However, the management never complained, for he was an extraordinary, irreplaceable artist. Of course one also appreciated that he did not live in such a way out of sheer wantonness, but rather in order to perfect his art and remain in constant practice.

Besides, it was quite salubrious up there; when, during the warmer seasons the side windows all around the theatre dome were flung open, and both fresh air and brilliant sunshine streamed in powerfully to break the twilight, it was indeed beautiful there. Certainly his human relationships were curtailed; only sometimes a fellow acrobat climbed up the rope ladder to him, they then sat on the trapeze, leaning right and left on the tether to converse; or the builders repairing the roof, exchanged a few words with him through an open window; or the fireman inspecting the emergency lighting in the top galleries called out to him respectfully, though incomprehensibly. Otherwise, all was calm and still around him; perhaps sometimes a theatre hand, having lost his way in the empty gallery, gazed thoughtfully up high, where the trapeze artist, unaware that he was being observed, practiced his art or rested.

The trapeze artist would have continued to live undisturbed in this fashion, had it not been for the inevitable journeys from place to place, that were extremely strenuous for him. Indeed, the ringmaster ensured that the trapeze artist would be spared from any unnecessary prolongation of his sufferings; to cross the cities one needed racing cars with which one could drive at great speed through the empty streets at night or in the earliest hours of the morning, but admittedly even that was too slow for the artist's longing for his home. On the train, a whole compartment was reserved in which he spent the entire journey up in the luggage holdall, so he could at least find as a sorry reward a replacement of sorts for his other lifestyle. In the next town on their circuit, the trapeze was already set-up in the theatre a long time before his arrival, all the doors leading to the theatre were thrown open, every aisle left free; but as ever, the most beautiful spectacle in the life of the ringmaster was when the artist set foot on the ladder and in no time, at long last, went up on his trapeze and hung aloft. Though such journeys – many as they were – had been satisfactorily arranged by the ringmaster, every new one was still an embarrassment for him, for apart from everything else, they unsettled the trapeze artist's nerves.

Once when they were again travelling together, the artist lying in the luggage holdall dreaming, the ringmaster leaning on the side of the window reading a book, the trapeze artist started to talk to him in a low voice. The ringmaster stood immediately at his service. Biting his lip the artist said he should now have two trapezes for his act, instead of his former single one …he should now have two trapezes opposite each other. The ringmaster agreed immediately; but the trapeze artist, as if wanting to prove that his acquiescence as well as his objection would be meaningless, said that he would never again and under no circumstances perform on only one trapeze. The very notion that it could perhaps happen once, made him shudder. Hesitantly and watchfully, the ringmaster declared once more his full agreement that two trapezes would be better than one; this new arrangement would make the production even more interesting and varied. At this point, the trapeze artist suddenly burst into tears. Deeply horrified, the ringmaster sprang to his feet, asking what had happened; getting no answer, he went up onto the holdall, caressed the artist, comforted him cheek to cheek and in so doing his own face was overflowed by the trapeze artist's tears. Only after cajoling him with so many questions did the trapeze artist say sobbing: 'Just this one trapeze-bar in my hands – how can I then go on living!' It was now already easier for the ringmaster to console him; he promised to immediately send a telegram from the next station in order to rig-up a second trapeze in the first town on the circuit. He reproached himself for letting the artist work on only one trapeze for such a long time, thanking and lauding him profusely for having finally made him aware of his mistake. Thus the ringmaster succeeded in gradually appeasing the trapeze artist and so returned to his corner. However, he himself was not serene; terribly concerned, he observed the trapeze artist surreptitiously, across the carriage, from over the top of his book. When such thoughts began to torture him once, could they ever completely come to an end? Would they rather increase? Would they not threaten his existence? Indeed, the ringmaster believed he saw the first wrinkles appearing on the smooth childlike forehead of the trapeze artist, apparently deep in sleep, after the weeping had stopped.

INTERPRETATION

A desperate appeal from a lonely soul – hidden away in the safe and serene pursuit of perfection for his beloved art, choosing to be confined within a solitary existence – now reaching out for the comforting companionship of another, revealing the true extent of his *First Sorrow*! This lonesome figure, devoted to his work, dedicated to an art form that sees him perched high above all others, as he remains so far removed from the world around, striving for absolute perfection, and though seemingly fulfilled, is so desperately unsettled, inconsolable in his despair, tortured by a restlessness no one understands; and yet, he knows more than any other, that his solitary existence has brought him to one undeniable conclusion, which must be ...what meaning do all his endeavours have without another to share them with? It is difficult to know whether this refers to the trapeze artist ...or Kafka himself!

The story speaks of an art-form which is one of the most difficult to master... that of the circus trapeze, highlighting the plight of a lone performer who had arranged his lifestyle in such a way that ...so long as he worked for the same company he could remain aloft on his trapeze, by day or by night: Initially, this was undertaken purely in pursuit of perfection, but gradually it turned into an unbreakable ritual. Did Kafka consider himself a trapeze artist in this way? With his literary art-form being one of the most challenging a person could aspire to, performed at a much higher level than any other, practiced high above the realms of the spectators below, where he organised his life in such a way that he could work and remain on his literary perch: Though this was initially undertaken in order to perfect his writing skills, it later became a necessary ritual. The modest needs of the trapeze artist were met by the use of a specially constructed container that sent up what he needed and was lowered with whatever he no longer wanted. Were Kafka's modest needs satisfied in the same way, with experiences and inspirations sent up to nourish him, his stories passed back down, and all through the specially constructed container which constituted his work?

Though the artist's way of living caused no problems for the other theatre people, as he remained quietly aloft during the turns of those acts, he did occasionally draw a stray glance from a member of the audience, which could be mildly unsettling for the other performers on stage: The management recognised that this artist was extraordinary and irreplaceable, they therefore chose to overlook this problem; for they knew the need for perfection was the sole reason for his need to stay at his post. This may suggest that Kafka's literary approach caused no problems for the other writers of the day, as he remained quietly on his writer's perch, watching them take their turns in the limelight: Although he may have drawn an occasional glance from the literary audience – which became an unsettling distraction at times – the fraternity elected to overlook this because they could see he was a rare and extraordinary writer, whose lifestyle was chosen in pursuit of excellence …not just to be a mere annoyance!

The artist found this lifestyle beneficial to his health, for during the warmer periods the high windows of the theatre could be opened to let in fresh air and sunshine, which only added to the allure of the place; though his social interaction was virtually non-existent, with only the occasional acrobat climbing up to spend some time with him, or the tradesmen working in the immediate vicinity sharing a few words, nothing broke the serenity of his peaceful domain. Did Kafka's artistic temperament find this way of living most healthful, with the warmer periods reflecting his most productive spells, when he would open the windows of his mind to let in fresh air and sunshine to brighten his mood? His social life was limited by his devotion to his literary station, as only those who would ascend into the lofty heights of his domain would truly be able to share his conversation. Perhaps Kafka recognised that he attracted the attention of certain members of the literary establishment as they 'gazed thoughtfully up high' at him

...as he 'practiced his art or rested', unaware he was being watched.

The trapeze artist could have happily continued this lifestyle were it not for the stressful journeys he had to take as part of his work; though the ringmaster made every effort to limit the discomfort to the artist, providing racing automobiles to speed the unsettled performer through the empty streets in the early hours, the artist simply could not get back to his post quickly enough. Does Kafka imply that his literary temperament could have contentedly remained at its literary perch had it not been for the stressful journeys he himself had to take, pulling his writer's instinct away from its station? Kafka may have tried to soothe his literary beast by speeding its journey back to the place it loved most – his literary trapeze – as quickly as possible in the early hours of the morning. However, railway journeys required a different approach, for the ringmaster reserved an entire compartment for his precious artist, who spent his time up in the luggage holdall as a form of consolation for missing his home: Before the artist's arrival in the next town the trapeze was already in place, all doors left open and gangways kept clear so he could immediately ascend to his station once more. Did Kafka now have to adopt a different strategy when travelling, as he was forced to store his literary temperament away like luggage until he arrived; only then could he ensure the doors to his creativity were left open... and the aisles of his mind kept clear, as he once again ascended into his literary heaven... to hang aloft in contentment.

The moment of truth arrives for the artist – and the ringmaster as well – during one of their train journeys, when the artist suddenly breaks his silence and demands another trapeze for his act. The ringmaster complies immediately, but the trapeze artist unexpectedly begins to cry, which horrifies the ringmaster who rushes to console his companion; only after much careful questioning from the ringmaster does the artist finally reveal that he feels his life has no point with only one trapeze to work with. Is this Kafka's temperament choosing to no longer remain taciturnly stored away – awaiting its arrival to yet another performance in a limited capacity – but instead unburdening itself to its master? This temperament demands its own metaphorical trapezes, the first... to continue its art, the second ...a medium through which to share its work; the ringmaster's immediate attention suggests Kafka's instant acknowledgement of his literary performer, recognising that he must comply with his own uniquely talented inner artist and appease it by occasionally publishing some of his work. The artist suddenly bursting into tears may reveal the frustration of Kafka's literary temperament, as it realises that to create but not to share serves little purpose, reflected in the line 'only this one bar in my hands – how can I then go on living!' The ringmaster surrendered to the artist's demands, just as Kafka would have surrendered to the demands of his temperament by publishing some of his work; however, despite satisfying the artist's needs, the ringmaster could not rest easily, for the unsettling feeling that troubled him and his artiste ...is the very same every author must feel when their temperament displays distress!

THE TRUTH ABOUT SANCHO PANZA

In the course of the years, Sancho Panza, who by the way never boasted about it, managed to deflect from himself the demon he later called Don Quixote. He did this by feeding him a great number of adventurous exploits, at all hours, evenings and nights; so much so that his demon then set out on the most uninhibited insane adventures which however, for the lack of a predetermined object that should have been Sancho Panza himself, harmed nobody. Sancho Panza, a free man, followed Don Quixote on his crusades, calmly and with equanimity, perhaps out of a certain sense of responsibility, and he had from this, an incredible and fulfilling time to the end of his days.

INTERPRETATION

Sancho Panza is a character in Don Miguel de Cervantes Saavedra's fictional story written in 1602. He is a peasant who becomes a companion to Don Quixote, following him on many adventures and helping him out of a number of conflicts. He followed Quixote out of duty and the promise of reward in the form of governance of his own island one day. The characters Sancho Panza and Don Quixote are considered to be a representation of reality over idealism, with the first keeping one's practical perspective in focus, whilst the latter nurtures hopefulness.

Kafka's parable elucidates the effect Don Quixote had on Sancho Panza, referring to him as Panza's 'demon'... most certainly due to the influence he held over the unwitting peasant: Don Quixote appears to possess Sancho Panza, who followed him stoically and loyally. Could it be that Kafka considered himself in

117

a similar role as Sancho Panza, the embodiment of reality, with his creative spirit illustrated by Don Quixote ...an instrument of hopeful idealism? Thus turning Kafka into the dutiful servant to his adventurous master!

It is written that, over many years and with modest intent, Sancho Panza managed to spare himself from the dangerous influence whom he referred to as Don Quixote; his course of avoiding such troubles – at all hours of the evenings and nights – was managed only through providing exciting exploits to satisfy his hungry demon. This could so aptly reflect Kafka's existence, as he succeeded over the course of many years by providing his literary demon with a great number of adventures... and all undertaken throughout many an evening into the late hours: Feeding his demon with great adventures allowed him to use his idealistic bravery and daring to court his art, whilst simultaneously making no boast of it... hence the limited amount published. Kafka may have noted how critical it was to satisfy the needs of his literary demon, appreciating that to starve such a hungry beast would leave him unable to channel his restless creative energy.

Sancho Panza's demon set forth on these incredible escapades without a specific purpose, though the goal should have been Panza himself, these adventures harmed nobody. Is this Kafka's admission that he too permitted his demon to undertake the most peculiar literary exploits possible? Though the object should have been himself, his writing instead concentrated on satisfying the needs of his beast of burden; despite this, his work harmed nobody. The free man that Sancho Panza was, allowed him to follow Don Quixote on his crusades, which he did willingly and happily, for these adventures gave him great pleasure throughout and until the end of his days. Kafka's conclusion suggests that he was more of a willing participant in the exploits of his demon's adventures then a possessed servant to an unrelenting master, and he too had an incredible and fulfilling time of it …to the end of his days.

Are we a Sancho Panza to our Don Quixote, pursuing, as well as nurturing, the hopeful idealism that craves adventure and could give us great satisfaction throughout our lives until the end of our days? Everyone's Sancho Panza requires a Don Quixote and vice-versa, as the balance between realism and idealism is vital for true contentment: Where realism keeps us grounded in our day to day existence, idealism is the escape we hope to aspire to …one day!

THE TEST

I am a servant, but there is no job for me there. I am timid and do not make inroads, I certainly do not make inroads in a line-up with other people; however, this is only one reason for my not being in service; it is also possible that this has nothing to do at all with my not being employed, anyhow, the principal reason is the fact that I am not being called to serve, others have been called and have thus not applied any more, or perhaps they simply have not had the desire to be called, whereas I, at least, have often felt this desire very strongly.

I therefore lie on the plank bed in the servants' quarters, stare at the beams on the ceiling, fall asleep, wake up, and fall asleep once more. Now and again I go across to the alehouse, where a sour beer is served, occasionally I have even reluctantly spilt a glass, but then again I drink. I gladly sit there, for from behind the closed little window, I can observe the windows of our house without anyone being able to detect me. I suppose one can certainly not see much, sitting here across the street, just the windows of the corridor; and furthermore, not those corridors which lead to the masters' apartments. It is even possible that I am mistaken, but somebody once, without me having asked, suggested that... and the general impression of the house front confirms this. Seldom do they open the windows, and when that happens, a servant does that, and he then leans against the parapet to look down for a while. There are also corridors where he cannot be caught off-guard. By the way I am not acquainted with these servants; those who are permanently employed upstairs sleep elsewhere, not in my quarters.

Once, when I arrived at the tavern, another guest was already sitting at my vantage point. I did not dare to look at him and wanted to turn around and walk away. The guest however called me over; it turned out that he was also a servant, whom I had seen somewhere, but until then not talked to. "Why do you want to run away? Sit here and have a drink. I will pay for it". So I sat down. He asked me a few things, but I did not have the answers. In truth, I did not even understand the questions. I therefore said: 'Perhaps you regret having invited me, I should go then,' and I wanted to stand up. He stretched his hand across the table and pushed me down: "Stay", he said. "That was only a test. He who cannot answer the questions has passed the test".

INTERPRETATION

What role should we adopt in life, what purpose do we serve, how can we make a worthy contribution to others, as well as bring fulfilment to our own lives in the process? These questions, probably the most poignant anybody may ask …set the foundation of *The Test*. Perhaps these were the very same questions Franz Kafka asked himself, as he restlessly searched for answers, for the role he needed to play and the contribution he had to make.

The predicament of the main character is one that can affect so many; choosing a role that neither values devotion nor fulfils potential. The protagonist claims he is a servant, but there is no work available for him, and furthermore… he does not push himself forwards to get any, so, despite his strong desire to serve…he does not. Here, more often than not, one is trapped chasing a role that simply does not exist: Though the character may believe this particular goal is the right one to pursue, the reality of the situation is that the role simply is not there to be taken: This should in itself make him consider whether his time and energy would be more appropriately directed looking elsewhere to fulfil his desire to serve. The protagonist complains that others have been called to serve, and without great effort; he however, believes he has tried harder, and longed to be called into service more than any other. The turmoil this character must feel! He yearns to serve, but at the same time, lacks the necessary confidence to push himself forwards; thus he will be destined to watch others fulfil this duty ...while he squanders his time. Perhaps his need to serve is a genuinely heartfelt feeling, but the present role he pursues does not appear to be the right choice for him; should he take his unfulfilled pursuits as a sign that it is time for a change?

Did Kafka view himself and his literature in this very same light? Yearning to fulfil a literary duty, feeling a need for his work to be of service to others, but at the same time... lacking the confidence to push himself forwards, desperately wishing to satisfy this need but instead standing back and watching others – who he believes have not tried as hard nor wanted it as much – take up this role.

The protagonist is therefore forced to spend much of his time in the servants' quarters, lying on a plank bed, occasionally drifting in and out of a slumberous state, or staring lackadaisically at the ceiling. This time spent idle... is a time spent tortured, for what other purpose can this character fulfil when he has nothing but time – without any direction – apart from wasting it sleeping or daydreaming. A life without purpose, or more importantly the right purpose, can so easily lead one to languish in a lethargic existence, draining one's valuable enthusiasm and energy. He escapes the monotonous confines of the servants' quarters by occasionally visiting the alehouse across from his dwelling; he can see the main house from there, and secretly watches the servants who mill about in the corridors; however, despite his alehouse distraction, he does not always savour the beer, claiming he occasionally spills a glass. This offers little comfort to a tortured soul, with both alehouse and beer bringing no respite from the dwelling and his enduring obsession to serve there: Yet again he hides away, inconsolable, fantasising about that which he appears to have no experience of, and knows so little about; does he prefer to live in his illusion instead of reality – allowing his life to stagnate as he makes no progress – continuing to claim so much but offer so little? Even the beer brings no pleasure; unlike most who go to the alehouse to quench their thirst, he admits to pouring the occasional glass away: These pleasurable indulgences are there to be savoured, relieving the stress ...if only briefly, allowing us to unburden ourselves, if only for a while. To find no enjoyment in such sweet nectars must surely be because he has lost his thirst for life!

Did Kafka find himself occasionally pouring away the sweet nectar of life, mostly taking it in, but rarely savouring it?

As he sits at his observation post, intrigued, watching the main house and the servants who wander through the corridors, his compulsion keeps his attention transfixed, despite knowing so little about that place. He concedes the servants and the corridors they wander through, are completely unfamiliar to him, for he does not share the same quarters, nor has he ever had the opportunity to walk through these corridors. This character's compelling obsession draws him toward the corridors of the main house, though he readily admits he knows nothing of where they lead: For their dullness is apparent, the monotony only broken when a servant opens a window to lean out, and even then... no great feat to be witnessed. Then the fateful day arrives when the protagonist visits the alehouse ...only to find another patron sitting in his usual seat; he wishes to turn and go ...but the stranger questions him, offering to buy him a drink and asking him to stay; though the queries are unanswered by the protagonist, the stranger remarks he has passed *The Test*. This fateful encounter may be the catalyst for much needed change in the protagonist's life; for the stranger may have raised the questions that he had not had the foresight to ask himself, thus setting a test to seek fresh answers ...and so explore new horizons.

Is this yet another reflection by Kafka, where the stranger setting the test is actually Kafka's truth setting a test for him, asking questions which he has no answers for, but compelling him to seek the answers to his predicament? The author may not only be telling us a tale of a character, but the tale of his character: Reflecting on his trials and tribulations so as to share with the world his uniquely enigmatic style that is purely ...Kafkaesque!

The Test is as relevant in modern life as it may have been to Kafka. The roles we choose for ourselves in life define and shape our existence. It is therefore crucial to question these role choices from time to time, to see whether they serve our best needs... or merely an imaginary and convenient purpose. In life we may come into contact with others who provide an insight into opportunities for change, it appears to be destiny's way of guiding us. When such people ask those essential questions, do we already claim to have the answers...or can we meet *The Test*, admit we do not always know ...and ask new questions that could help us move forwards?

THE STREET WINDOW

Whoever leads a lonesome life yet longs to connect now and then... whoever, according to changes in times of the day, the weather, occupational affairs and the like ...on the spur of the moment just wishes to see an arm, any arm, to hold onto, cannot pursue that for long...without a street window. It can also be that he does not seek anything at all, that he only rests on the windowsill, a tired man, his eyes turning to and fro, from the public to the heavens; or he does not want to look out at all, having tipped the head slightly backwards. Nevertheless, from down below, the horses, with their retinue of carriages and noise, drag him at last into the human harmony.

INTERPRETATION

This unusually brief parable feels more akin to a throwaway remark than what one might consider a short story: Could anyone argue with the straightforward logic of the narrator ...reminding us that if we wish to engage with life around, we will need a window to look through onto the street below? Probably not! However, suppose the window he speaks of is not a window to the street... but a window from the soul? Rather than a mere architectural feature of a room looking out, it is instead, a reflection of the eyes that take in the vision that lays before us...the window through which we view the world around!

Those who live a reclusive lifestyle may seek comfort in the peace and quiet of solitude: Choosing this existence because they find little or no joy in the bland conversation and tedious routine of their fellow citizens; nor might they find enjoyment in the aggressive nature of so many modern attitudes... or the frenetic pace of city-living. It is in this seclusion, as they shy away from the world outside... that they feel most at ease, relaxed and productive without any disharmonious intervention. There may also be those who are forced into a solitary existence, abandoned, either because they are considered a burden which simply serves no purpose: Such isolation can compound the feelings of loneliness, causing greater seclusion.

Whether Kafka was highlighting his own plight or that of other solitary souls, one thing appears to ring true ...that the need to make a connection with the world around exists at the heart of our basic instincts. Even when we become distracted by our thoughts and daydreams, or are simply too afraid to engage with others for fear of more heartache, our natural inclination draws us to the animated energy around. So how can we make this connection despite such desperate isolation? The answer may lie in the need to maintain one's Openness at all times, extend a hand and share the generosity of one's spirit.

Whether the window belongs to a building from which we gaze out at the street, or is the Openness in our heart...both are viewing platforms which maintain lines of communication. For regardless of the time of day, the weather, the state of our business, or the circumstances that affect us, it is the humanity around that draws us towards it: Only through a window from the soul can one reach out ...to the street!

JACKALS AND ARABS

We encamped in the oasis. My companions were asleep. An Arab, tall and white, sauntered past me; he had been attending to the camels and was making his way to the sleeping quarters.

I threw myself down on my back in the grass; I wanted to sleep; I could not; the plaintive cries of a jackal came from afar; I sat up again, and what appeared so remote, suddenly became so close. A swarm of jackals encircled me, with matt golden lifeless eyes, their lean bodies moving swiftly… similar to that of a cracking whip.

One came from behind, pushing against my arm, so close as if it needed my warmth; it then walked in front of me and started to speak, virtually eye to eye: "I am the oldest jackal, known far and wide. I am pleased to be able to greet you here. I had almost lost hope, for we have been waiting endlessly for you. My mother had waited for you, and her mother and before her all the mothers down to the mother of all jackals, believe it!"

'That surprises me,' I said, forgetting to kindle the pile of logs which lay ready, so as to ward off the jackals. 'I am very surprised to hear that. It is only by chance that I have come here from the far North, and I am supposed to stay only a short time. What do you jackals want then?'

As if encouraged by my perhaps too friendly reception, they tightened their circle around me; their breath was short and panting.

"We know", began the eldest, "that you come from the North, in fact we are basing our hopes on that. The wits that cannot be found here amongst the Arabs, exist over there. You know, no spark of reason could be struck out of their cold arrogance. They kill animals to eat, but despise carrion".

'Don't talk so loud', I said, 'there are Arabs sleeping in the vicinity'.

"You are indeed a stranger," said the jackal, "otherwise you would have known that never in the history of the world, has a jackal been frightened by an Arab. Why should we be frightened of them? Is it not our great misfortune that we are outcasts amongst them?"

'Could be, could be', I said, 'I do not pass judgement on things that are far out of my league; seems as if this is an ancient dispute, it is probably in the blood and perhaps, will end up in blood as well'.

"You are very clever," said the old jackal; and they all started to pant faster, their lungs pumping energetically, though they were staying still; a foul smell, which one could bear only with gritted teeth, was oozing out of their open mouths. "You are very clever; what you said conforms to what our ancient teachers have related. We will take their blood and thus the quarrel will end".

'Oh!' I exclaimed, more zealously than I intended, 'they will fight you; they will shoot you down in numbers with their rifles'.

"You misunderstand us", he said, "as is the fashion of human beings, encountered even in the far North. We will certainly not kill them. The Nile would not have enough water to wash us clean. We will indeed flee even from the mere sight of their living flesh, into cleaner air, into the desert which is for this reason our homeland".

All the jackals around and those too who had arrived from the remotest places, lowered their heads in between their forelegs and wiped them clean with their paws; it was as if they wanted to conceal a repugnance so terrible, that I felt the urge to leap out of their circle and flee.

'What do you intend to do then?' said I, trying to stand up; but I could not; two of the young animals behind me had sunken their teeth firmly into my jacket and shirt; I had to remain seated. "They are train-bearers", explained the old jackal earnestly. "A testimony of honour". 'They must let go of me,' I cried out to the old jackal, and also to the young ones who had turned around. "Of course they will," said the old one, "if that is your wish; in a little while though, for as is our tradition, they have sunken their teeth so deep that they will have to unclench their jaws gradually. In the meantime, please hear our request". 'Your behaviour has not made me very receptive,' I said. "Do not let our clumsiness influence you against us," he said; and now for the first time his voice turned into a natural tone of lament, seeking help. "We are poor animals, we only have our teeth; for whatever deed, good or bad, we only have our teeth". 'Well, what do you actually want?' I asked, a little mollified.

"Sir," he cried out, and all the jackals started to howl; in the farthest of the far, that could have sounded like a melody. "Sir, you should end this quarrel that divides the world. You are the one our forefathers had described, the one who will accomplish this task. We must have peace from the Arabs; air to breathe; our view of the horizon should be cleansed of them; no cries of a sheep butchered by an Arab; all creatures should perish in serenity; we should be able to cleanse them out of their flesh and empty their blood, with no interference. We want cleanliness, nothing but cleanliness" – and at this they all shed tears, they all sobbed – "how can you bear to live in this world, O noble heart, O sweet bowels? Dirt is their white; dirt is their black; their beard is dread; one would want to spit at the mere sight of their eyes; and hell breaks out of their armpit when they lift their arm; and so my lord, so my dearest Sir, by means of your powerful hands, by means of your all powerful hands, cut their throats with these scissors!" At a jerk of his head a jackal approached holding a little old pair of rusty sewing scissors in his fangs.

"Well, at last the scissors and with that, the end!" Cried the Arab guide of our caravan who had sneaked up to us upwind and was now wielding a gigantic whip.

The creatures all fled in haste, but remained at a distance, huddled close to each other, so close and stiff that they looked as if penned and surrounded by will-O-the wisps.

"Well Sir, you have now seen and heard this spectacle," said the Arab laughing as heartily as the natural reticence of his tribe would allow. 'Do you know then what these beasts want?' I asked.

"Of course Sir," said he. "It is indeed well known; as long as there are Arabs, these scissors will wander through the deserts, and will roam with us to the end of our days. They will offer the great job to every European; every European is just the right one to be appointed. These animals have a nonsensical hope; fools, they are real fools. Nonetheless we love them; they are our dogs, lovelier than any of yours. Look now, a camel perished last night, I have had it brought here".

Four Arabs came forth and threw the hefty carcass before us. Hardly was it thrown down when the jackals raised their voices. As if each were irresistibly drawn by a cord, they closed in, haltingly, streaking the floor with their bodies. They had forgotten the Arabs, forgotten their hatred, the effacing presence of the rotten cadaver enthralled them. One had already seized the throat and found the artery with the first bite. Just like a small frenzied engine that desperately wants to extinguish an overpowering fire, the jackal twitched and thrashed every muscle of his body; and soon all piled up on the carcass, engaged in the same task.

Now the guide started forcefully wielding his powerful lash from all sides on them; they raised their heads; half inebriated, almost unconscious; they saw the Arab standing before them; felt the lash sting their muzzles; leapt back and ran a length. The blood of the camel remained there in a pool, reeking upwards, the carcass was torn open in several places. They could not resist; they came back again; the guide raised his whip once more; I took hold of his arm.

"You are right Sir," he said, "we will let them do their job; it is also time to decamp. You have indeed seen them. Wonderful creatures, aren't they? And how they hate us!"

INTERPRETATION

The devious and deceptive nature of those who prey on the naivety of others, as they aspire to win their trust, in order to manipulate their actions, appears to be at the heart of *Jackals and Arabs*. These underhanded individuals can appear at any time, in any place, and in many guises, as they seek out unwary souls to prey on. Kafka ingeniously sets the scene and circumstances for his protagonist, as the wary stranger who passes through a barren desert, entrusts his safe passage solely to that of his Arab guide, only to find himself the centre of attention for a pack of insidious creatures.

The protagonist's caravan encamps in the Oasis; though the traveller tries to lie back and rest, he is unable to, as his peace is disturbed by the distant howl of a jackal; then quite unexpectedly he is surrounded by a pack of the creatures, who move in en-masse, trapping their unsuspecting victim. Does Kafka suggest that at those times when we take refuge in our own metaphorical oasis – wherever this may be – we inadvertently let our guard down, allowing our jackals the opportunity to strike; what may initially appear to be only a distant hint of danger, can quickly close in on us unexpectedly, as we become imprisoned in their trap.

The head jackal addresses the bewildered traveller, exclaiming his pleasure to meet him and assuring the stranger that they have been awaiting his arrival; a wait endured since the time of their forefathers. Here Kafka illustrates the cunning and deceptive nature of our jackals, with their calm and respectful approach,

133

appearing humble and sincere as they introduce themselves, making us feel important as they inform us that we are their saviours; though this is not enough, for they also endeavour to reassure us of their truthfulness. The traveller is surprised by this admission from the head jackal; at which point he remembers he should have rekindled the logs that would have kept the beasts at bay; Kafka reminds us of how easily we can be taken by surprise by these deceptive characters, especially when we forget to keep the fires of our of awareness alight …so as to keep our beasts at bay.

The traveller reveals too readily that he is from the North, and appears to show too keen an interest in the jackals' plight. The lead jackal exploits the traveller's innocent admission of his arrival from the North, claiming he was already aware of this, for he based his hopes on it. Does Kafka demonstrate how readily we can be drawn into our jackals' game, as we become too comfortable in their company and reveal too much about ourselves, which only encourages them to exploit the situation further? The lead jackal continues to flatter the traveller, noting his intelligence over the Arabs; the beast then uses this opportunity to condemn the Arabs, sullying their character. How our jackals use these cleverly deceptive methods that appeal to our vanity by praising us, whilst condemning their adversaries in the same breath: With such a ingenious tactic, is it any wonder we could be tempted to give credence to our jackals' story… especially as they are so generous with their flattery!

The Traveller appears to weaken to the Jackals' appeal, as he expresses his concern that the Arabs may overhear them; the lead jackal responds by assuring the traveller of their fearlessness, remarking that it is their misfortune to be banished amongst the Arabs. Kafka reveals yet another cunning strategy employed by our jackals, as they draw us into their game, awaiting our interest and concern for their plight, demonstrating their courage, whilst making themselves out to be unfortunate victims of their predicament; this clever trick inspires the unwary participant to respect the deceiver for his bravery, whilst being encouraged to feel sympathy for his apparent misfortune. The traveller believes the disharmony between the Arabs and the jackals to be a serious one indeed, and one where blood will need to be spilt in order to conclude their feud: Though the jackal agrees with the traveller's conclusion, he quickly deflects the responsibility for this task away from himself and the pack... which responds with a unified display of disgust. It appears that the jackals' every remark and gesture compound their credibility in the eyes of the stranger, as they play out their game, waiting for the perfect moment to reveal their true intention.

The traveller's intrigue prompts his enquiry as to what these beasts propose to do, though he is also aware of his own predicament – confined within the clutches of the jackals – and so tries to get up, but is firmly held down by two others; the traveller insists that he is to be released from their hold, and is assured he will be, however, it will take time for the beasts to loosen their grip. This illustrates how curiosity compels us to seek answers from our jackals, and how, despite our aversion to their company, we are held captive by their insistence: The desperate actions our deceivers are willing to take when they feel we may escape, as they pin us down for as long as they can ...determined to succeed with their plans. The lead jackal makes his appeal, imploring the traveller to undertake the task they wish for so greatly, and return peace and harmony back to the desert; he remarks that all creatures shall pass away peacefully, allowing them to feast on the remains without interference from the Arabs. Now the genuine reason for the jackals' hatred of the Arabs and their motive for wanting them vanquished becomes apparent; they do not wish to protect the other animals from the Arabs, but instead wish to take back dominion of the desert and eliminate their competition for food.

The jackal goes further in his condemnation of the Arabs, condemning their cleanliness and telling the traveller of the disgust they feel at even a glimpse of an Arab; how readily our jackals contrive criticism of their adversaries, seeking even more sympathy, as they play the role of the victim so well! The small rusty pair of scissors the jackals produce for the traveller to use as a weapon is then brought forward; this unimpressive rusty implement is no great weapon worthy for the mighty task of the jackals: Kafka may use such a simple implement to symbolise the tool of choice they try to arm us with, not necessarily a mighty weapon with which to perform their task, but one none-the-less dangerous enough to the unsuspecting recipient, and conveniently placed at our feet.

The Arab guide steps in at this point, interrupting the jackals before they present the traveller with the scissors; he informs the traveller that the jackals seek the assistance of every European for their great task, assuring them they are the right person to undertake this job; adding that as long as the Arabs exist so will the scissors; it appears to be the nature of the jackals to always plot against the Arabs and seek the help of unwary strangers. This suggests how our deceitful creatures constantly exploit every opportunity to gain advantage, as their persistence accompanies us throughout our lives. The Arab tells the traveller that these dogs are fools, but it is for this reason they are considered to be their dogs, with none finer found anywhere. Kafka suggests our positive influences are accompanied throughout life by corresponding negative ones; this serves to validate the importance of the former, as the latter mendaciously plots against it. The Arab then brings a camel's carcass for the Jackals, watching them feast on it before lashing them to show his power, thus illustrating how our positive influences willingly feed their negative counterparts out of compassion, but ultimately have the power to assert control. The Arab concludes by remarking how wonderful he thinks the jackals are, but recognises how much they hate the Arabs: Does Kafka imply that even the positive influences must surely admire the perseverance and cunning of the negative entities; for their determination to exploit every opportunity, regardless of how many times their efforts are thwarted ...deserves at least acknowledgement of respect?!

What was it that inspired Kafka to write *Jackals and Arabs*: Did he encounter his own Jackals in life, deceitful charlatans who befriended him, trying to persuade him to use his literature to promote their cause and harm their adversaries? Did the Arabs reflect Kafka's literary confidence, providing the guidance and protection he needed as he crossed the barren deserts of his turbulent mind? Were the jackals Kafka's enemies, who constantly plotted to exploit him for their own benefit? Could the small rusty pair of scissors symbolise the weapon that is ever present and dangerous, though not impressive nor ever used, none-the-less the tool someone else chooses for Kafka to use on their behalf? Or did Kafka take shelter on many an occasion in his own fertile oasis of creativity, wondering through the barren deserts of his uninspired periods; as he lays back to rest in this oasis, his Jackals appear out of nowhere to try to kill off his creative confidence.

Jackals and Arabs forewarns about the exploitative nature of deceptive forces that appear suddenly in our life, and alerts us to be vigilant. When we relax in our oasis, and forget to rekindle the fires of awareness that protects us, we leave ourselves vulnerable: For our jackals will try anything and everything to gain our compliant servitude... from pleas and appeals to impress us, to pinning us down in hope of eventually arming us with their weapon of choice, so that we will perform their underhanded task, whilst they remain blameless. Let us always revel in our oasis, and thrive in its sanctuary, but be constantly vigilant, never allowing our Jackals to encircle us unexpectedly; let us always maintain the fires of awareness to ward off the beasts before they make their play, and so ensure that we do not become a pawn in another person's dangerous game.

REJECTION

When I meet a beautiful girl and plead with her: 'Be ever so kind as to come with me'… and she silently passes by, this is what she implies:

"You are no Duke with a highfaluting name, you are no broad-shouldered American with a Red Indian stature and level dreamy eyes, with a skin seasoned by the breeze of grasslands and watered by flowing rivers, you have not travelled to and over the oceans which are unknown to me and which I would be unable to find. So I ask, why should I, such a beautiful maiden, go with you?"

'You forget, no automobile speedily chauffeurs you through the streets, swaying you in long thrusts; I do not see any retinue of gentlemen in tight tailored suits courting you, gathered in a crescent …pursuing you, and whispering pleasantries; your breasts are well restrained in that bodice, but your thighs and hips compensate for the confinement; you are wearing a pleated taffeta dress, and how it absolutely enchanted us all…last autumn! And you rightly smile – beckoning mortal danger upon yourself – from time to time.'

'Yes, we are both in the right… and not to confront the truth of it, we would each rather go home alone, wouldn't we?'

INTERPRETATION

The pain of rejection, a cutting blow to any recipient …leaving its wound upon our mortal frame: The scar from which …it is up to us, how deep shall be this mark that will remain!

The initial interest and excitement that spring forth from our amorous curiosity in another can all too quickly be crushed by a dismissive remark or a scornful reaction. Whether the rejection comes in the form of a verbal rebuttal or simply a silent snub, either can provoke our insecurities into goading us, playing on our waning self-confidence as we are now overwhelmed by strong feelings of inadequacy. Could this parable be a revelation by Kafka about his own first-hand experience of rejection? Such a direct theme possesses a personal feel... unlike his usual unconventional objectivity cloaked in surrealism.

The narrator's overactive imagination appears to get the better of him... and so very quickly as well; despite the girl silently passing him by, he immediately believes he has been ignored simply because he does not match up to an imaginary ideal she is looking for. He does not consider for even a second, that maybe it is his approach that fails to capture her interest ...much less her heart; to 'beg her,' and then expect her to go with him after such a request, would be a preposterous notion for any self-respecting lady, especially with this complete stranger. The narrator's imagination carries him off on an unfounded tangent, as he believes he is not wealthy nor experienced, not well travelled nor daring enough for her; this exemplifies how quickly our thoughts can change when we allow rationality to escape from our reasoning! More importantly, even if her snub meant exactly what he thought, what right had he to expect her acceptance? His free choice allows him to make his less than heroic appeal; surely her free choice permits her to ignore such a pathetic plea, and accept if she so chooses... or not as the case may be!

Ironically, her rejection causes him to become dejected and reject her in turn: The frustrations of his bruised ego now sniping criticism at the girl, with unpleasant comments about her solitary demeanour and appearance. Surely it would have been more pleasant for him to accept the fated outcome of their paths crossing and go on his way... without such immature behaviour to spoil his mood? Bizarrely, he concludes with "Yes, we are both in the right and not to confront the truth of it, we would each rather go home alone, wouldn't we?"...and all this exaggerated out of proportion and instigated simply by one quiet girl who chose to say nothing! Maybe, if he had been less desperate in his plea, with more intelligence in his approach, the outcome could have been so very different: Unless he recognises these shortcomings, he may be destined to continue the cycle of rejection, adding to his misery and bitterness …forcing him to always go home alone!

METAMORPHOSIS

PART 1

Upon waking from unsettled dreams... Gregor Samsa discovered as he lay in bed, that he had been transformed into a giant insect: Lying on his armour-like hard back he raised his head a little and saw his curved, brown belly, the surface divided in arched, stiff joints, from the top of which the blanket was gliding downwards and he could scarcely keep a hold of it. His many legs, puny and pathetic in comparison with his girth, flickered helplessly before his eyes. 'What is happening to me?' he thought. This was no dream. His room, a proper but rather small human one, was still located within the four familiar walls. On the table, an assortment of drapery samples were spread pell-mell – Samsa was a traveller – and a picture that he had recently cut out of an illustrated magazine was placed in a pretty, golden frame. It represented a lady clad in a fur hat and a fur stole, sitting upright and holding out to the onlooker a heavy fur muff into which vanished her whole forearms.

Gregor's eyes turned next to the window and the murky weather – one could hear the raindrops thud against the window panes – which made him feel quite melancholy. 'How would it be, if I went on sleeping a bit longer and forgot all about this foolishness?' he thought; but that was totally unfeasible, for he was accustomed to sleeping on his right side and in his present state he was unable to adopt this posture. However forcefully he threw himself to the right side, he swayed once again onto his back. He tried that probably a hundred times, closing his eyes, not to have to see his wriggly legs, and did not stop until he started feeling a light, dull pain, never experienced before in his sides. 'Oh God,' he thought, 'what an arduous job I have chosen! Day-in, day-out on the road. The commotions are a great deal more than the business at home; besides this plague of constant travelling there are also further worries to contend with…train connections, the irregular unsavoury food, the socializing with people which is ever changing, never lasting, never sincere. To hell with the entire thing!' He felt a slight itch on top of his belly; then thrust himself on his back slowly nearer to the bedpost in order to raise his head more easily; he found where his itch was located, covered by nothing but little white dots, which he could not make sense of; he wanted to touch this place with one leg, though he soon pulled back since the contact provoked shivers in him.

He glided back into his earlier position. 'This early rising,' he thought, 'makes one truly idiotic. A person should have a good sleep. Other travellers live like harem women. When I for instance, go back to the inn mid-morning, in order to rewrite the acquired orders, these gentlemen have just sat down for breakfast. I should try that with my boss; I would be thrown out of my job on the spot …after all, who knows, if that would not be a good thing. Had I not been held back by my parents, I would have resigned long ago, I would have gone to the boss and told him exactly what I thought, from the bottom of my heart. That would make him fall off his desk! He has an odd way of perching on his desktop and talking down to the employees who moreover, have to come quite close to him since he is hard of hearing. Well, the situation is not completely hopeless; once I have put the money together and paid back my parents' debt to him – that could still take five or six years – I shall definitely do this. I will cut myself completely free. In the meantime I must get up, for my train leaves at five'.

Gregor looked across at the alarm clock that was ticking on the cabinet. 'Good God!' he thought. It was six thirty and the clock hands were moving quietly onwards, it was actually past the half hour and approaching a quarter to. The clock had perhaps already gone off? One could see from the bed that it was correctly set for four o'clock; it had certainly rung. Yes, but would it have been possible to sleep smoothly through this strident ringing? Well, he had not slept smoothly, but in all likelihood very solidly; but what is he to do now? The next train would leave at seven o'clock; to catch it, he would have to hurry like mad and he had not even packed up the samples, and he himself did not feel thoroughly fresh and nimble. Even if he could catch the train, the boss's outburst would be unavoidable, for the shop's manservant would have been waiting for the five o'clock train, and announced his failure to turn up long since. He was a true servant of the boss, weak and gullible. What if he now called in sick? But that would be extremely embarrassing and suspicious, for during his five years of service Gregor had not been ill once. For sure the chief would arrive with the health insurance doctor, reproaching his parents for the laziness of their son and ignore all arguments on the advice of this doctor – who considered every employee to be in perfect health but perpetually work-shy. In fact, in this case, would he be so wrong? Incidentally, Gregor, apart from an unnecessary drowsiness, a consequence of his lengthy slumber, felt good and quite ravenous.

As he was mulling over these thoughts with great haste, unable to decide whether to leave his bed – the clock struck quarter to seven – there was a gentle knock on the door next to the headboard of his bed. 'Gregor', someone shouted – it was his mother – 'didn't you have to go away?' 'Oh the gentle voice!' Gregor panicked as he heard the sound of his own voice answering, unmistakably his own but mixed with a burdensome, painful, squeaking undertone which caused the words to lose their clarity…literally in the first minute, and then the lingering sound so corrupted the sense that it was impossible to know whether one had heard it well. Gregor wanted to answer and explain everything at length but under the circumstances limited himself to say: 'yes, yes, thank you Mother, I am getting up now'. Passing through the wooden door, the change in Gregor's voice was not noticeable outside, for the mother was reassured with this explanation and shuffled away. But through this short conversation the other members of the family had become aware that Gregor, against expectation, was still at home, and the father was knocking on one of the side doors, feebly but with his fist. 'Gregor, Gregor,' he shouted out, 'what is it then?' And after a short while he urged him again but with a deeper voice: 'Gregor! Gregor!' From behind the other side door the sister asked plaintively: 'Gregor? Are you not well? Do you need something?' Gregor responded to both: 'I am almost ready,' trying to make his voice sound as normal as possible, accurately pronouncing each word and taking long pauses between them.

The father returned to his breakfast, but the sister whispered: 'Gregor, I beg you, open the door'. However, Gregor was not at all thinking about opening the door, and he rather complimented his own foresight, acquired through travelling, to always locking the doors at home during the night. To begin with, he wanted to get up quietly and without being disturbed, put his clothes on and above all have breakfast; only then could he consider what to do next; for he indeed realised that by cogitating in bed he would never reach a reasonable conclusion. He remembered the occasional pain he had been feeling, perhaps due to him lying awkwardly in bed, which upon getting up had revealed itself to be a figment of his imagination; he was now eager to see how his imaginary ailments would gradually dissipate. That the change of his voice was nothing other than the precursor to a heavy cold, an occupational hazard of commercial travellers, he had absolutely no doubt. To shed the blanket was easy enough; he only needed to puff himself up a little, and it fell off by itself. But to go further was more difficult, mainly because he was so unusually wide. He would have needed many arms and hands to set himself upright; instead he only had these little legs which moreover, were constantly moving uncontrollably in all directions. He tried once to bend one of them and that was the first that straightened itself, and when he at last succeeded in achieving what he wanted with this leg, all the other little legs began wriggling wildly in a painful frenzy. 'It is useless to remain in bed,' thought Gregor. Initially, he wanted to get out of bed with the lower part of his body; but the lower part – which he had not yet seen and from which he had no perception – proved difficult to move; everything was going so slowly; and as he finally, having been driven to despair, threw himself forwards, forcefully and recklessly, he misjudged the angle, bumped quite forcefully into the lower bedpost, and the burning pain he now felt, taught him that the lower part of his body was currently perhaps the most sensitive.

He therefore tried to first get his upper body out, and carefully turned his head towards the edge of the bed. He succeeded easily in doing that and despite its weight and breadth, the mass of his body slowly followed the turn of the head. As he at last freed his head out of the bed in the open air, he took fright to continue in this manner, for if he finally were to fall over, it would take a miracle to avoid injuring his head. Critically, if he were to lose consciousness now…he would rather remain in bed. As he lay there, sighing, and watching his little legs fighting each other more angrily than before, if this were at all possible, finding no prospect to bring order and tranquillity in this arbitrariness, he told himself again that he could not possibly remain in bed and that it would be most reasonable to sacrifice everything and free himself, even if there were only a glimmer of hope in doing so. At the same time however, he reminded himself, that quiet reflection and the quietest reflection is even more preferable than desperate resolutions.

In such moments he set his eyes as sharply as possible on the window, but unfortunately the sight of the morning fog which engulfed even the other side of the narrow street, gave him little confidence or buoyancy. 'Already seven o'clock,' he told himself

147

as he again heard the alarm clock go off, 'already seven o'clock and still such a fog'. He lay down quietly for a little while, breathing softly, perhaps awaiting the return of his real and natural circumstances. But he then told himself: 'Before it strikes a quarter past seven, I must leave this bed completely...without fail. Besides, by then someone will have come from the office to enquire after me, since the office opens before seven o'clock'. He now set about swinging the entire length of his body fully out of the bed. In case he fell down, his head, which he would sharply raise during the fall, would probably remain uninjured. His back seemed to be hard and was unlikely to be hurt if he fell on the carpet. His greatest worry was the loud noise that would most probably, if not horrify those behind the doors, at least arouse a lot of concern. But he had to risk it! As at least half of Gregor's body was already out of the bed – the new method was more of a game than a struggle, he needed more than ever to swing backwards – he realised how simple everything would be if someone came to his aid. Two strong people – he thought of his father and the maidservant – would have been quite sufficient; they would have pushed their arms under his arched back to prise him out of the bed, then bent down under his weight and merely stuck it out until he rolled and landed on the floor, where the little legs would hopefully acquire some significance. Now, apart from the fact that the doors were locked, should he really call out for help? Despite all the distress, he could not suppress a little smile at the thought of it.

He had already gotten so far that he could hardly keep his equilibrium as he swung sharply, and very soon he would have to finally decide – for in five minutes, it would be a quarter past seven – when there was a knock on the front door. 'This must be someone from the office,' he told himself and nearly froze, while his little legs began dancing ever more wildly. For a moment everything stayed still. 'They are not going to open' Gregor said to himself, grabbing at some nonsensical hopefulness. But then of course, as always, the maid walked to the door with firm strides and opened it. Gregor only needed to hear the visitor's first greeting words and he already knew who it was – the chief clerk himself. Why on earth was he condemned to serve in a firm, where one would come under deep suspicion by the smallest of lapses? Were the entire group of employees really so dim? Was there no single loyal devoted person amongst them, who having wasted a couple of hours not attending to the firm's business, would become so completely mad by feelings of guilt that he would virtually be unable to leave his bed? Didn't it suffice to just let an apprentice boy come over and enquire...was this enquiry at all necessary? Did the chief clerk himself have to come and thus demonstrate to the entire innocent family that the investigation of this suspicious affair could have been entrusted solely to him? And more as a result of the agitation that these reflections provoked in him, rather than as a consequence of a calculated decision, Gregor swayed out of bed with all his force. There was a loud thump, but not an actual crash.

There had not been a noticeable sound, partly because the impact of the fall was muffled by the carpet, and also because his back was much more resilient than Gregor had imagined. Only he had probably not held his head carefully enough, and therefore bashed it; he spun around and rubbed it on the carpet out of anger and pain. 'Something has fallen over there,' said the chief clerk in the side room on the left. Gregor tried to imagine whether something similar could one day happen to the boss as well; one should actually not dismiss such a possibility. But as if giving a crude answer to this question, the chief clerk took a few firm steps in the adjoining room and let his leather boots creak. From the right adjoining room, the sister whispered to inform Gregor: 'Gregor, the chief clerk is here'. 'I know,' said Gregor to himself; but he did not dare to raise his voice enough so that his sister could hear him. 'Gregor,' said the father now from the side room on the left, 'the chief clerk is here and is asking why you did not catch the early train. We do not know what we are supposed to tell him. Besides, he wants to talk to you personally, so please open the door. He will have the graciousness to excuse the disorder in the room'. 'Good morning, Mr. Samsa,' the chief clerk intervened amicably. 'He does not feel well,' said the mother to the boss, while the father was still busy talking outside the door; 'he is unwell Sir, believe me. Otherwise, why else would he miss the train? The boy has indeed nothing on his mind but your business. It actually infuriates me that he never goes out in the evening; he has now been eight days in town, but stayed home every single evening. He just sits there near us at the table, reading the newspaper or studying the railway schedules. For him, amusement means doing fretwork. Talking of that, he has for instance in the course of two or three evenings, carved a small frame. You would be surprised how pretty it is; it is hanging inside the room; you will see it as soon as Gregor opens the door. I am actually very happy that you are here, Sir; by ourselves, we could never have brought Gregor round to open the door; he is so stubborn; he is unwell for sure, even though he denied it this morning'. 'I will come out soon,' said Gregor, slowly and thoughtfully, but not moving in order not to lose a single word from the conversation. 'I could not have explained it any other way myself, dear lady,' said the chief clerk, 'hopefully it is nothing serious. On the other hand, if I am allowed to say, we business people – fortunately or unfortunately, if you will – should be able to just overcome a light discomfort, out of regard for the business'. 'So could the chief enter now?' asked the father impatiently, as he again knocked on the door. 'No,' said Gregor. A painful silence fell in the left side room; in the room on the right, his sister began to sob.

So why didn't the sister go to the other room? She had just gotten out of bed and had not yet begun to dress. Why was she crying then? Was it because he had not stood up and opened the door to let the chief enter? Or was it because he was in danger of losing his job? Or was it because the chief clerk will again harass his parents with his claims? For now, these were indeed unnecessary worries. Gregor was still here and did not have the slightest intention to leave his family behind. Currently, he preferred to lie on the carpet and nobody who would know his circumstances, would in all honesty have demanded that he let the chief in. Surely Gregor could not be instantly sent away just because of this little act of discourtesy, for which he would later find a convenient excuse. It seemed to him, that it would be a lot wiser to leave him in peace now, instead of disturbing him with tears or reasoning. But it was precisely the uncertainty that bemused the others and excused their behaviour. 'Mr. Samsa,' cried out the chief clerk raising his voice, 'what is the matter then? You barricade yourself there in your room, answer only by a simple "yes" or "no", create severe, unnecessary difficulties for your parents and neglect – incidentally, I mention this just in passing – neglect your business responsibilities in an outrageous manner. I am speaking here in the name of your parents and your boss, and am pleading with you quite genuinely to give us an immediate, clear explanation. I am astounded, I am astounded. I had always thought of you as a quiet, reasonable person and now it seems that you have started to flaunt some peculiar moods. In fact, the director indicated to me this morning a possible explanation for your oversight – it regards the fact that you have recently been entrusted the cash payments – but I put in my word of honour in all honesty and said that this account could not be accurate. However, now I have seen your inconceivable stubbornness, I have not got the least inclination to intervene on your behalf…and your position is definitely not the most solid. I had originally intended to tell you everything face to face, but since you have made me waste my time unnecessarily here, I cannot see why your parents should not witness it as well. Your achievements lately have been, well... very unsatisfactory; admittedly it is not the right season to accomplish a high level of business, that much we acknowledge; but not to achieve any business during the whole season, is not acceptable, and cannot be acceptable, Mr. Samsa'.

'But Sir,' cried out Gregor, beside himself and in the excitement of the moment forgetting everything, 'I will immediately, this very moment, open the door. Just a little indisposition...a dizzy spell has prevented me from getting up. I am still lying in bed. But now I feel already quite fresh. I am even coming out of bed. Just a little bit of patience! I am still not as well as I thought. But I feel better already. How could a man be struck down in such a manner! Just yesterday evening, I felt quite good, my parents could tell you that, better said, already yesterday evening I had a little premonition. One should have considered that. Why on earth have I not notified the firm! But one always thinks that the illness could be weathered out without staying at home. Sir, spare my parents! There is no basis at all for all you are reproaching me with now; no one had told me anything. Perhaps you have not read the last orders that I have sent in. Besides, I can still go to work with the eight o'clock train, these few hours of rest have made me stronger. Please Sir, do not let me hold you back; I shall be at work very soon, and please be kind enough to relay this to the director and recommend me to him'.

While Gregor was blurting out all this in haste, barely knowing what he was talking about, he approached the cabinet quite easily, perhaps as a result of the earlier exercises in bed; using it, he now tried to straighten himself up. In fact he wanted to open the door, let himself be seen and talk to the chief clerk; he was anxious to learn what the others who were so insistent to see him, would say at his sight. If they were horrified, then Gregor would have no more responsibility and could be in peace. But if they accepted everything calmly, then he also had no reason to be agitated and could in fact, if he hurried, be on the eight o'clock train. At first he slipped a few times on the smooth surface of the cabinet but he eventually swung around one last time and stood there upright; he did not pay any more attention to the pains and aches – as burning as they were – in his lower body. Now he let himself fall against the backrest of the nearest chair, the borders of which he clasped with his little legs. He had thereby achieved command over himself and he fell silent in order to hear the chief clerk.

'Did you understand a word of it?' asked the chief clerk, 'he is not taking us for fools, is he?' 'For God's sake no,' cried out the mother already in tears, 'he is perhaps seriously ill and we are tormenting him'. 'Grete! Grete!' she then shouted. 'Mother?' the sister called out from the other side. They communicated with each other across Gregor's room. 'You should at once go for the doctor. Gregor is ill...quickly for the doctor. Did you hear Gregor speak?' 'That was an animal's voice,' said the chief clerk in a remarkably faint tone in comparison with the mother's shriek. 'Anna! Anna!' shouted the father through the front room into the kitchen, clapping his hands. 'Get a locksmith immediately!' And already the two girls were running through the front room, swishing their frocks – how could the sister have gotten dressed so quickly? – then ripping the door open. There was no sound at all of the doors closing; they had in all likelihood left them open, as is the custom in houses where a great misfortune has occurred.

But Gregor had become much quieter. Of course one could not understand a word he was saying anymore, nevertheless these words sounded clear to him, clearer than before, perhaps as a result of his ear becoming accustomed to it. Regardless, everyone now believed that there was something wrong with him, and they were ready to help. The confidence and certainty with which the first steps were taken, did him good. He felt involved once again in the human cycle and hoped to get from both, the doctor and the locksmith – without really making any distinction between the two

– magnificent and astounding achievements. In order to attain the clearest voice possible for the forthcoming crucial meetings, he coughed a little, though anxious to keep it muffled, given that it could possibly ring differently than the sound of a human cough and for this he could not rely on his own judgement anymore. In the meantime, there was complete silence in the adjoining room. Perhaps the parents were sitting down at the table with the chief clerk whispering secretly, perhaps they were all leaning against the door, listening in.

Gregor shuffled slowly with the chair towards the door, relinquished it there, threw himself at the door and stood against it upright – the balls of his little feet were a little gummy – and rested a little while after all his exertions. He then set about turning the key in the lock. Unfortunately it seemed as if he had no proper teeth – how could he then grip the key? His jaws were certainly very strong and he used them to move the key, not heeding the fact that he had undoubtedly damaged something... for a brown liquid started oozing out of his mouth, flowing over the key, dripping onto the floor. 'Do listen now,' said the chief clerk in the side room, 'he is turning the key'. That was a great encouragement for Gregor; but they should all have called out to him, his mother and his father too: 'Come on Gregor' they should have shouted 'concentrate on the lock, one thing at a time!' And in the belief that all his efforts were being pursued with excitement, he unconsciously bit on the key with all his force.

As the key kept turning, he danced around the lock, holding himself upright only with the help of his mouth, and if necessary, he hung himself on the key or pressed it down again with the whole weight of his body. The loud click of the lock snapping back endlessly ...inspired Gregor positively. Taking a breath, he told himself: 'I did not actually need the locksmith' and he placed his head on the handle to open the door. Since he had to unlock the door in this manner, and it was actually wide open now, he could not yet be seen. He first had to slowly and indeed very carefully turn around the doorframe as he did not want to fall over clumsily on his back, upon entering the room. He was still toiling with that challenging move and did not have time to heed anything else, when he heard the chief clerk blurt out a loud 'Oh!' – it sounded like the rush of the wind – and he now saw him too, and how he, who was the nearest to the door, pressed his hand on his mouth and slowly flinched back, as if dispelling an invisible, consistent and effective energy. The mother – she stood there despite the presence of the chief clerk, with her dishevelled and ruffled hair from the night before – clasped her hands and first looked at the father, then took two steps towards Gregor and fell down amid her sprawling ample skirts, her face quite untraceable, sinking into her bosom. The father clenched his fist with a hostile expression as he attempted to push Gregor back into his room; he then looked around the front room uncertainly, covered his eyes with his hands and began sobbing so uncontrollably that his mighty chest heaved.

Gregor did not walk into the front room, he just leaned against the firmly bolted door frame from inside, so that only half his body was visible and on top of that his head, turning sideways, peeking over to see the others. In the meantime it had become much lighter. On the other side of the street one could clearly see a section of the endless, dark grey building opposite – it was a hospital – with its protruding, austere, regular windows; it was still raining, but now in large, particularly distinguishable drops falling literally one by one. The breakfast dishes were laid over abundantly on the table, for breakfast was the most important meal of the day for the father…he protracted it by reading different newspapers for hours. Just on the opposite wall hung a photo of Gregor at the time of his military service, depicting him as a lieutenant, with his hand on his sword, a carefree smile, demanding respect for his position and uniform. The door to the room was open and so was the front door, and one could see the courtyard and the top of the downward spiralling steps.

'Now,' said Gregor, thoroughly confident that he was the only one who had retained his calm, 'I will get dressed, pack up the samples and go off. Will you let me go? Will you? You see Sir, I am not stubborn and I work readily; travelling is troublesome, but I could not live without the travelling. Where are you going then, Sir? To the office? Yes? But will you relay everything truthfully? One could work ineptly for a while, but then that is the precise moment for remembering the previous achievements and to consider that later on, when the impediments will have been removed, one will certainly work more diligently and with better concentration. I am indeed so very indebted to the chief director, you are perfectly aware of that. By the same token I am very concerned about my parents and my sister. I am in great difficulty but I will work my way out of it again. But do not make it harder than it is for me. Please take my side in the office! They do not like travellers, I know that. They think they make a fortune and thereby lead fabulous lives. They do not even have a particular ground to reflect deeper on this prejudice. But you Sir, you have a better outlook on the affairs than the rest of the personnel, and said in complete confidence between us, a better outlook than even the director himself, who by virtue of his position as entrepreneur is easily misled in his judgement, to the disadvantage of the employees. You also know very well that the traveller, who spends the whole year outside the office, can so easily fall victim to gossip, hearsay and baseless grievances against which it is almost impossible for him to defend himself, for he is mainly completely unaware of them and only then, when he comes back home from a journey quite exhausted, does he feel the nasty consequences, without being able to trace their origin. Sir, please do not go away without telling me a word which will show me you at least admit I am a little bit in the right!'

But the chief clerk had already turned away as Gregor began uttering his first words, staring back at him with an open mouth, over a twitching shoulder. While Gregor was speaking, he had not stood still even for a moment, but inched away towards the door, without taking his eyes off Gregor, quite gradually, as if there existed a secret prohibition on leaving the room. He was already in the hallway and after the last sudden movement with which he had shuffled out of the living room, it seemed as if he had just burnt the soles of his feet. In the hallway however, he stretched his right arm away from himself towards the steps, as if an unearthly salvation were awaiting him. Gregor realised that he could in no way allow the chief clerk to depart in this mood, for his position in the office could be gravely jeopardized. His parents did not comprehend all that very well; over the years they had convinced themselves that Gregor's position in this firm was quite secure and had been so worried by the present troubles that every foresight was now lost on them.

But Gregor had the foresight. The chief clerk had to be held, reassured, convinced and finally won over; the future of Gregor and his family depended indeed on that! If only his sister had been here! She was clever; she had wept while Gregor was still quietly lying on his back. The chief clerk – such a ladies man – would have certainly let himself be steered by her; she would have shut the front door and would have reasoned with him in the living room and dissipated his fright. However, the sister was not there now and Gregor had to act himself; and without thinking that under his present circumstances, he could no longer move ...yes, without even thinking that his speech was again possibly – no, probably – incomprehensible, he let go of the doorframe. He thrust himself through the opening; he wanted to go up to the chief clerk who, funnily enough, was still clutching firmly with both hands, the railings of the landing. Now seeking a foothold, he immediately fell down, shrieking, on his many little legs. Soon after, he started feeling for the first time that morning, a physical sense of well-being; the little legs had a firm ground underneath; to his delight, they were becoming fully obedient; they even strived thereafter to carry him forth wherever he wanted; he was already starting to believe that the ultimate recovery from all his ailments was at hand. In the same instance, while he was still swaying due to his restricted movement, not too far from his mother who was lying on the floor, seemingly quite sunken down, she suddenly sprang up, arms outstretched, fingers splayed out, shrieking: 'Help, for God's sake help!' She held her head inclined, as if she wanted to see Gregor better, but contradictorily ran back, mindlessly; she had forgotten that the laid out table stood behind her; she sat on it, hastily and absent-mindedly and did not seem to notice at all that coffee started gushing out of a large knocked over jug, onto the carpet.

'Mother, mother,' said Gregor softly, looking up at her. For a moment, the chief clerk had completely slipped his mind; he could however not withhold from snapping away in the void, at the sight of the coffee streaming. His mother started screaming again, bolting away from the table and falling into the arms of the father who had rushed towards her. But Gregor had now no time for his parents; the chief clerk was already on the landing, pressing his chin on the railings and looking back for the last time. Gregor had one final go to outrun him as much as possible; the chief must have intuited that, for he leapt over several steps and disappeared. 'Huh!' and his shriek reverberated throughout the staircase. It appeared that the chief clerk's flight had now unfortunately completely confused the father who had remained composed so far; instead of chasing the chief himself or at least not hinder Gregor in his pursuit, he grabbed with his right hand the clerk's cane – which along with his coat and hat, he had left behind on an armchair – and with his left hand he took a large newspaper from the table and began stamping his feet, brandishing the cane and the newspaper in order to drive Gregor back into his room.

Gregor's pleas did not help him, they were not even understood and as he tried meekly to just turn his head, the father stamped his feet even harder. On the other side, the mother had opened a window quite wide, despite the cool weather; she leaned far outside the window and pressed her face into her hands. A strong cold draught arose from the street into the staircase, the curtains flew open, the newspapers on the table rustled and some pages were blown over the floor. The father was shoving and rushing relentlessly while hissing like a savage. Since Gregor was inexperienced in moving backwards, his retreat was painfully sluggish. If he could only turn around, he would soon be in his room, but he feared to enrage the father with his time consuming rotation, for at any moment he was threatened by a deadly blow falling on his back or head from the cane in his father's hand. Eventually however, Gregor had no alternative, since he realised to his horror that by walking backwards he could not even adhere to the correct direction. So he began rotating as swiftly as possible, but in reality quite slowly, and incessantly darting anxious looks towards his father. Perhaps the father noticed his good intention, for he did not disturb him in so doing; only now and then he conducted the turning movement from afar with the tip of his cane. If only the father could have stopped this unbearable hissing! It made Gregor go out of his mind. He had already turned completely around as he, listening as ever to the hissing sound, actually erred and turned slightly back again. He was happy when he eventually found himself before the doorway; it appeared however that his body was too wide to go through without further help.

Of course under his present circumstances it did not remotely occur to the father to push open the other door, in order to create an adequate passage for Gregor. He was merely fixated on the idea that Gregor should go back into his room as rapidly as possible. He would not have allowed the intricate preparations that Gregor needed in order to stand upright and thus succeed in passing through the doorframe; instead he urged Gregor to move forwards now that there were no impediments, under a great deal of noise; the voice behind Gregor did not sound like his own father's; now this was no joke, and Gregor thrust himself forward – come what may – into the doorway. One side of his body heaved, he lay lopsided in the doorway, one of his shoulders totally chafed, there remained ugly stains on the white door; soon he became stuck and could not move, the little legs hung from one side quivering in the air; the others hurt when pressed against the floor – then the father gave him a veritable redeeming push from behind and he flew, bleeding severely, far into his room. The door was pushed shut with a blow of the cane, and then everything finally fell quiet.

PART 2

Early in the morning, it was in fact still quite dark, Gregor had the opportunity to test the strength of the decisions he had just made, for his sister, fully dressed, opened the door of the living room and peeked in. She did not find him immediately but as she noticed him under the sofa – God, he must be somewhere, he could not have flown away – she was so terrified, that she, not being able to control herself, slammed the door shut again. Regretting her behaviour, she immediately opened the door once more and walked in on tiptoe, as if she were visiting a seriously ill person or even a stranger. Gregor had pushed his head forward precisely to the edge of the sofa and was observing her. Would she notice that he had left the milk untouched – certainly not for the lack of hunger – and would she bring in some other food which would suit him better? If she did not do that of her own initiative, he would rather starve than draw her attention to it; nevertheless he actually had a tremendous urge to dash forward from under the sofa, throw himself at his sister's feet and beg her for something good to eat. But the sister noticed at once, with amazement, that the bowl was still full and only a few drops of milk were spilt all around; she promptly picked it up, though not with her bare hands, rather with a rag, and took it out.

Gregor was extremely curious to see what she would bring to replace it…and thought about several possibilities. He could never have guessed though, what his sister really did next, in her kindness. She brought him a selection of food to test his taste and she laid them all on a sheet of old newspaper. There were half rotten vegetables; bones from the previous night's dinner, covered by a thick white sauce; a few raisins and almonds; a piece of cheese that Gregor had declared unpalatable just two days before; some dry bread, one buttered roll and another buttered and salted. Furthermore, she placed a bowl next to the food. She filled this pan, which in all likelihood was going to belong exclusively to Gregor, with water. Sensitively, since she knew Gregor would not eat in front of her, she quickly moved away and even locked the door so that Gregor could feel as relaxed and comfortable as he needed. Gregor's little legs whirred as he now went up to the food. Incidentally, his wounds must have completely healed by now, he did not feel any hindrance, he marvelled at and thought about how he had more than a month ago, cut himself on the finger with a knife, and how that little sore was still hurting up until the day before. 'Am I now going to be less sensitive?' he thought, while sucking avidly on the cheese which had overwhelmingly attracted him more than any other food. Rapidly, and one after the other, he devoured the cheese, the vegetables and the sauce ...the satisfaction brought tears to his eyes. By contrast he did not like the fresh food at all; he just could not bear the smell and he even hauled the stuff he wanted to eat a bit further from the rest. He had already long finished and was lazing at the same place, when the sister thinking that he had probably retreated, slowly turned the key in the lock. This startled him, even though he had been dozing, he rushed once again under the sofa.

But it took a great deal of self control, even if it was only for a short time, to stay under the sofa while his sister was in the room, for the rich food he had eaten had bloated him somewhat and he could barely breathe in that narrow space. Almost choking and with tears welling up in his eyes, he watched how his unsuspecting sister not only swept together the leftovers, but also the food that he had not even touched, as if she knew they would not be needed anymore; and he saw how she hastily tipped it all into a bucket, covered it up with a wooden lid, whereupon she carried everything out. She had barely turned around and gone when Gregor came out from under the sofa, stretched and puffed himself out. Gregor now obtained his daily food in this manner, once in the morning, while the parents and the maid were still sleeping, and the second time after everybody had finished their lunch, this was because the parents then took a nap again and the maid would be sent away by the sister to carry out an errand. No doubt they did not wish Gregor to starve either, but perhaps they could not have endured seeing how he was eating and preferred to hear of it from the sister, or perhaps his sister wanted to spare them more grief, for they had been indeed suffering enough.

Gregor could not discover from anyone at all, with which excuse the doctor and the locksmith were gotten rid of on that first afternoon; because no one could understand him, everyone, even his sister, assumed he could not understand them either; therefore he had to settle for hearing his sister now and again sobbing or invoking the saints, whenever she was in his room. It was not until later, as she had become more accustomed to the circumstances – of course there had never been a question about complete understanding – that Gregor sometimes snatched a comment that was meant as friendly or at least could have been so interpreted. 'Seems that he liked the food today,' she said, when Gregor had eaten up all his food, and when on the contrary he did not touch it, which was becoming increasingly the case, she used to repeat with sadness 'Everything has been left again'. Though Gregor could not obtain much news directly, many a time he could overhear a lot from the side rooms and as soon as he heard a voice, he would run to the door in question and press his whole body against it. In the early days especially, there was no conversation, without his case being discussed one way or another, even if only secretly.

For two days, at all meal times, consultation was going on about how best to handle the situation; but even between meal times one talked about the same subject, for there were always at least two members of the family around, given that no one felt like staying at home alone but at the same time no one wished to leave the house for good. Even the housemaid – it was not quite clear how much she knew about what had happened – had right from the first day begged the mother, on her knees, to dismiss her at once, and when a quarter of an hour later she told her goodbyes, tearfully giving thanks for her dismissal as if it were the greatest blessing bestowed on her, she made an awesome pledge, without being asked for it, not to betray the slightest detail of what had happened, ever, to anyone.

Now the sister had to cook as well, together with the mother; this certainly didn't cause too much hassle, since the family did not eat much anyway. Gregor kept hearing one or the other of them offer food in vain, with the only answer always being: 'Thank you, I've had enough,' or something similar. Not much was drunk either. Occasionally the sister would ask if the father wanted a beer and affectionately offer to fetch it herself, and as he kept silent, she said, so that she would spare him any concerns, that the concierge could get it...but then the father would pronounce a strong 'No' ...and no word would be spoken thereafter. As early as the first

163

days the father exposed the whole financial prospects to the mother and the sister. From time to time he would get up and take out some vouchers and receipts that were held in his small safe, which he had salvaged after the failure of his business five years earlier. One could hear how he opened the complicated lock, and after withdrawing what he wanted, locked it again. The father's account was the most gratifying statement Gregor had heard since his imprisonment.

He had always believed that nothing had remained from the family business, at least his father had told him nothing to the contrary, and certainly Gregor had not asked him anything about it either. Gregor had always strived to make his family forget the business failures which had brought them so much heartache and despair. Back then, he had started to work with a particular fervour and from being a simple clerk he had become a commercial traveller overnight, naturally with higher financial possibilities; the result of his toil was immediately converted into cash that would be laid on the table at home, to the astonishment and joy of the whole family. Those were happy days and they were never ever to be repeated, not with such lustre anyway, even though later on, Gregor made so much money that he could and did shoulder the expenses of the whole family. Everyone including Gregor himself had gotten used to that; the family was thankful to receive the money and Gregor was glad to provide it, however, no particularly warm gratitude was ever bestowed. Only the sister had still remained close to Gregor and since she, unlike himself, loved music very much and played the violin movingly, his secret plan was to send her to the academy of music, notwithstanding the high costs, which he would raise one way or the other.

Occasionally, during his brief stays in town, the academy would be mentioned in the course of the conversation with his sister, but always as sort of a beautiful dream, never to be attained, and the parents certainly did not appreciate even an innocent mention of that. However, Gregor thought about it quite determinedly and planned to announce it ceremoniously on Christmas Eve. These futile thoughts, especially in his present circumstances, went through his mind as he remained there upright, clinging to the door and trying to listen in. Sometimes he could not listen out of exhaustion and would carelessly let his head drop against the door; but then he would immediately hold it up firmly again, since the slight noise thus provoked, would be heard on the other side and prompt everyone to fall silent. 'What is he is trying to do now?' said the father after a short while, clearly turning towards the door... and only then would the interrupted conversation gradually gather pace again.

Gregor heard and learnt enough to realise – for the father repeated his explanations often, partly because he had not been acquainted with the business for a long time now and partly because his mother could not grasp the meaning of his account the first time around – that despite their great mishap, there certainly still remained a small fortune at hand which in the meantime had even grown slightly, due to the accumulated untouched interest. Apart from that, the money that Gregor had brought home every month – he had only ever kept a few guilders for himself – had not been entirely used up and now amounted to a small sum of capital on its own. Behind the closed door, Gregor nodded fervently, delighted with such unexpected foresight and thrift. He could certainly have paid off his father's debts to the chief director with this surplus money and the day he could have resigned would have come sooner... but now things were undoubtedly better off left the way his father had arranged.

Yet this money was by no means sufficient to let the family live on its interest; it could perhaps keep them afloat for one, or at most two years, but no more. It was simply a sum that one should not actually touch but keep for an emergency; the money for the livelihood had to be earned. However, now the father, though healthy indeed, was an elderly man who had not been working for the past five years and at any rate could not be much trusted in business. During these five years of leisure, the first in his arduous and certainly unsuccessful life, he had put on a lot of weight and become quite sluggish. Or perhaps would his elderly mother who suffered from asthma, for whom just walking around the house was troublesome and who every other day ended up breathless on the sofa near the window, now have to earn money? And his sister, still a child at seventeen, who until now had been so pampered, had always dressed well, slept long, helped out a little at home, allowed herself a few modest treats and above all played the violin? When the conversation turned to the necessity of earning money, Gregor always let go of the door and threw himself on the cool leather sofa nearby, for he became hot from shame and sorrow.

He often lay there the whole night, did not sleep at all and scraped the leather for hours; or he heartened himself for the great effort of pushing an armchair to the window, crawling up on it to lean on the window sill, clearly trying to recapture the memory of the liberating feeling of looking out of the window. Actually, with each day passing, he could see even the not too distant things ever more indistinctly; the hospital opposite whose all too common aspect he had cursed earlier became completely blurred, and had he not been certain that he lived in the quiet but heavily urbanised Charlotten Street, he could have believed to be looking out on a wasteland, in which the grey sky and the grey earth conjoined indistinguishably. His vigilant sister must have seen only twice that the armchair stood next to the window, and from then on, every time she tidied the room, she pushed the armchair right up to the window and she even left the inner window casements open.

Had Gregor only been able to speak to his sister and thank her for everything she was doing for him, he could have borne the burden of her services more easily and would have not suffered so much. She certainly tried to blur the embarrassment of the whole thing as much as possible and of course the more time that passed, the easier it all became for her. With the passage of time, Gregor came to see through everything much more accurately as well. He found the very way she entered truly horrible. Whereas in the past she wanted to spare everyone from looking into Gregor's room, now, barely had she entered that she would rush straight to the window without taking the time to shut the door, would open it wide with hasty hands as if she were suffocating and stay by the window a short while, even when it was freezing, taking deep breaths. She terrified Gregor with the running and the noise, twice a day; the whole time he quivered under the sofa and was well aware that she would certainly have spared him, if it had been at all possible for her to stay in the same room as Gregor, with the windows closed.

Once, a month after Gregor's metamorphosis, when there was certainly no more reason for the sister to be astonished by Gregor's appearance, she arrived a bit earlier than usual, to find Gregor immobile and rigid from fright, looking out of the window. He would not have been surprised if she had not entered, since by his very position, he prevented her from rushing to open the window, however, not only did she not enter, she instead ran back and locked the door. A stranger would have simply thought that he intended to ambush and bite her. Of course Gregor hid at once under the sofa but he had to wait until mid-day for her to come back and this time, she appeared much more uneasy than usual. He realised thereof that his appearance was still unbearable for her and that she indeed had to fight with herself not to run away from the sight of even the smallest parts of the body that stuck out from beneath the sofa. In order to spare her from this sight, he carried some bed linen to the sofa – the whole process took him four hours – and arranged it in such a way that he was completely covered by the sheet and even if his sister bent down, she could not see him.

Had she thought the bed linen was not necessary, she could have easily taken it away, for it was quite clear Gregor had not closed himself off for his enjoyment; but she left the bed linen as it was and Gregor even believed to have snatched a glimpse of a grateful look in her eyes, as he carefully lifted the sheet in order to see how his sister had received the new set-up.

For the first fortnight the parents felt unable to bring themselves round to visit him, and one could hear often, how they fully acknowledged the current endeavours of his sister, whereas before, they had often gotten angry with her; for they thought of her as quite a useless young girl. However now, both father and mother often waited outside Gregor's room while the sister was tidying inside and as soon as she walked out, she had to explain in detail what it looked like in the room, what Gregor had eaten, how he had behaved this time and whether there had been a slight improvement. Incidentally, the mother wished to visit him relatively soon but the father and sister dissuaded her on rational grounds which Gregor listened to attentively and entirely approved. Later though, they had to hold her back by force and as she then cried out: 'let me go to Gregor, he is my unfortunate son! Can't you understand that I have to go to him?' Gregor thought it might be better if she came to visit him, of course not every day, but perhaps a couple of times a week; she understood everything much better than his sister, who despite her courage, was still a child and after all she may have undertaken such an arduous task purely out of childish flippancy.

Gregor's wish to see his mother soon materialised. Out of consideration for his parents he did not want to be seen by the window; at the same time he was unable to crawl too far on the few square meters of flooring, he found quietly lying down at night unbearable and the food did not give him the least pleasure anymore and so, in order to break the monotony, he took to crawling criss-cross over the walls and up on the ceiling. He particularly liked to hang from the ceiling; it was so much better than lying on the floor. He could breathe freer; a light quiver would run through his body; and up there, in his almost jubilant absent-mindedness, sometimes to his own astonishment, he would let go and crash on the floor. Of course he was now much more in command of his body than before and such a big fall did not harm him. His sister soon noticed the new entertainment that Gregor had invented for himself – by crawling he left behind traces of his sticky substance – and so she set her mind to remove the furniture, mainly the cabinet and the writing desk which hindered his movements, so as to make it possible for Gregor to crawl in as wide a space as available. However, she was unable to do this alone; she did not dare to call on the father for help; the housemaid most certainly would not have helped her, for this seventeen year old girl had courageously persevered after the dismissal of the previous cook, but had asked as perquisite, to keep the kitchen perpetually shut down and opened only when called upon on special occasions; so the sister was left with no other alternative than calling on her mother in the absence of the father.

Proclaiming her rousing delight, the mother came round but fell silent at the door of Gregor's room. First the sister peeked in to verify if everything was in order; only then did she let the mother enter. Gregor hastily pulled on the sheet and folded it even deeper and the whole thing looked like bed linen that had been randomly thrown on the sofa. This time Gregor forbore to spy from under the blanket; he renounced to see his mother and was only delighted that she had come at all. "Come on then, one cannot see him", said the sister, obviously guiding her mother in by the hand. Gregor now heard two weak women trying to move two heavy old pieces of furniture and his sister continually taking on the larger part of the work, not heeding the warnings of the mother who feared she would be overstrained. It took a long time. After a quarter of an hour the mother suggested they had better leave the cabinet; for, firstly, it was too heavy and they would not be ready before the father's return and by leaving it in the middle of the room they could obstruct Gregor's movement; secondly, it was not at all certain that by removing the furniture they would be doing Gregor a favour. To her, the contrary seemed to be the case; the sight of the empty walls aggrieved her; and why wouldn't Gregor have the same sentiment, given that he had been accustomed to this furniture for a long time and could therefore find himself unhappy in an empty room.

'And does that not mean... ' concluded the mother, very quietly, as if in a whisper, as if wanting to avoid Gregor – whose exact whereabouts she did not know – hearing even the sound of her voice, for she was convinced he could understand nothing of what she was saying, 'does that not mean that by removing the furniture we would indicate to him that we have lost every hope for his recovery and that we have abandoned him ruthlessly to himself? I think it would be best if we kept the room in exactly the same condition as it was before, so that when Gregor comes back to us, he finds everything unchanged and thus forgets easier what had in the meantime happened'.

On hearing his mother's words, Gregor realised that the lack of immediate human communication, along with a monotonous family life in the course of the past two months, must have confused his mind, for otherwise he could not justify how he should have genuinely desired his room to be cleared out. Did he really fancy letting that warm, cosy room furnished with inherited pieces, be transformed into a den where he could crawl about freely and undisturbed, with simultaneous, swift and complete oblivion to his human past? Was he now indeed so close to forgetting, and did only the voice of his mother which he had not heard in a long time...arouse him? Nothing should be removed; everything had to stay; he could not forego the beneficial impact of the furniture on his condition; and if the furnishings were to hinder his pointless crawling about, that would not be a drawback, but rather a huge advantage.

Unfortunately, his sister was of a different opinion. In discussions with her parents, she had become accustomed, indeed not wholly without justification, to behave like an expert in matters concerning Gregor and so now, the mother's advice was for her reason enough to remove not only the cabinet and the writing desk – originally her own decision – but rather the entire furnishings, with the exception of the sofa which was indispensable. This was of course not an act of childish defiance, nor an unexpected and hard-won self-confidence she had lately acquired and exhibited, as a result of this challenge; she had actually observed that Gregor needed a lot of space for crawling and as far as she could tell, there was no need for any furniture at all.

But perhaps the quixotic spirit of young girls her age played a role, a spirit that seeks its gratification in every opportunity, and which now enticed Grete to transform Gregor's room into a horrifying place, so that she could perform more than she had until now; for no other person apart from Grete would dare to walk into a room, where Gregor alone ruled over the empty walls.

So she did not let her mother, who seemed quite uneasy in this room, dissuade her from her resolve. The mother soon fell silent and began helping Grete in moving out the cabinet, to the best of her abilities. Well, Gregor could probably do without the cabinet if need be, but the writing desk absolutely had to stay. The women had barely left the room with the cabinet which they had, groaning and moaning, pushed out, than Gregor stuck his head out from beneath the sofa in order to see how he could best intervene, with utmost caution and care. Unfortunately it was his mother who first reappeared, while in the adjoining room, Grete was clasping the cabinet and swinging it alone, back and forth, unable to control it. But the mother was not accustomed to Gregor's appearance and he could have sickened her; so Gregor, horrified, rushed back to the other end of the sofa and in so doing could not prevent the sheet from moving slightly at the very front. That was enough to alert his mother. She faltered, stood still for a moment and then ran back to Grete.

Though Gregor kept repeating to himself that nothing unusual had happened apart from a few pieces of furniture being moved around, it turned out, as he soon had to admit, that all the to-ing and fro-ing of the women, their little cries and the scraping sounds of the furnishings on the floor, created a hubbub that surrounded him from all sides, making him pull his head and legs into a knot, press his body onto the floor ... and inevitably forced him to say that the whole thing was unbearable for him. They cleared out his room and took everything that was dear to him; they had already moved out the cabinet where he kept the fret saw and various work tools. They had loosened the writing desk which was dug into the floor and on which he had written assignments as a university, high school and even primary school student. He had no more time to assess the intentions of the two women whose existence he had forgotten, since exhausted, they were now working in complete silence and only the heavy toddle of their feet could be heard.

So he burst out – the women were leaning against the writing desk in the adjoining room, to take a breather – changing his direction four times. He did not exactly know what he intended to salvage first; then he saw hanging on the already naked wall the striking picture of a fur clad lady. He rushed and latched onto the glass which soothed his hot belly.

Gregor was now completely concealing the picture and at least no one could take it away anymore. He contorted his head towards the door in order to observe the women, as they returned to the room.

They had not allowed themselves much time for a rest and came back after a short while; Grete had placed her arm around the mother and was almost sustaining her. 'Now then, what else do we take?' said Grete, looking around the room. Her eyes locked in with Gregor's on the wall. She maintained her composure, probably due to the presence of the mother; she bent her face towards the mother in order to prevent her from looking around and said, rash and shaking: 'Come, shall we go to the living room for a while?' Grete's intention was quite clear to Gregor. She wanted to take the mother safely away, before chasing him off the wall. Well, anyway, she could at least try to do that! He sat on the picture and did not yield. He would rather leap into Grete's face.

But Grete's words had only unsettled the mother, she remained to one side, caught sight of the enormous brown blotch on the flowery carpet and screamed – before her consciousness actually realised that, what she had seen was Gregor – in a shrill, raucous voice: 'Oh God! Oh God!' and fell on the sofa with outstretched arms as if she had given up everything, and did not move anymore. 'Hey Gregor!' shouted the sister with a raised fist and forceful look. Since the metamorphosis, these were the first words she had directly spoken to him. She ran to the side room to fetch some aromatic essence with which to bring her mother round. Gregor wanted to help as well – there was still enough time to salvage the picture – but he was stuck firmly to the glass and had to break away by force; he too then ran to the side room to see whether he could give his sister some advice, like in the old times; but he had to stand idle behind her, while she rummaged through various phials; as she turned around the sight of him frightened her, a phial fell on the floor and broke into pieces; a splinter injured Gregor in the face; it was some caustic medicine splashed on him; Grete then took as many phials as she could carry and without delay ran back to her mother; she slammed the door shut with her foot. Now Gregor was locked out of the room where his mother, perhaps through his fault, was close to death. He dared not open the door since he did not want to scare away his sister who had to stay with their mother; now he had nothing to do but wait. Crushed by self-reproach and worries, he began crawling all over the place, on the walls, the furniture, the ceiling, and in the end he fell in the middle of the large table, as in his despair, the whole room seemed to be spinning around him. Gregor lay there flat on his back for a short while; everything was quiet around him and perhaps that was a good sign. Then the doorbell rang. The housemaid had of course locked herself in the kitchen and Grete had therefore to go and open the door. The father had arrived. 'What's happened?' were his first words; Grete's appearance had indeed betrayed everything to him. She answered with a dull tone, obviously pressing her face on her father's chest. 'Mother fainted but she is already better. Gregor has broken loose and is out'. 'I was expecting this of course,' said the father, 'I had told you so many times, but you women never want to listen'. It was clear to Gregor that the father had misunderstood Grete's all too short disclosure and had assumed that Gregor was guilty of some serious misconduct. Therefore he now had to try and placate his father, since he had neither the time nor the possibility to enlighten him. So he fled to his room and pressed himself against the door, so that the father, upon entering from the hallway could immediately see that Gregor had the best of intentions to return to his room at once and that there was no need to drive him back, but instead, they only needed to open the door and he would disappear.

The father was not in the mood to notice such thoughtful gestures. 'Ah!' he cried out at once upon entering, with a tone denoting both rage and joy. Gregor drew his head back from the door and raised it towards his father. In reality he had not imagined him, as he now was. In recent times he had certainly been too busy crawling about and had neglected the rest of the house and he would now have to be prepared to meet with some changed state of affairs. Yet, yet, was this man really his father?

The same man who used to lie buried in his bed, every time Gregor came back from a business trip; who on the evening of his return, received him wearing his dressing gown, sitting in his armchair; who was quite unable to stand up and would only raise his arms to show his pleasure; who on the rare occasions they went on a stroll as a family – one or two Sundays a year or on some very important holidays – walked between Gregor and his mother, even slower than them, wrapped up in an old overcoat, cautiously using a crooked walking stick to make his way forward; who when he wanted to say something, almost always stood still and gathered his entourage around him; was this the same man? But now here he was, steadfastly upright, clad in a stiff blue uniform with golden buttons, like the one bankers wear; his hefty double chin was protruding out of his jacket's high stiff collar; from under his bushy eyebrows, the fresh and vigilant gaze of his black eyes darted through; his usually dishevelled white hair was parted and styled in an embarrassingly luminous shade. He threw his cap which had a gold monogram affixed – probably that of some bank – across the room on the sofa and walked towards Gregor, the tail-ends of his long jacket thrown back, his hands in his trouser pockets, his face dogged and combative. He probably had not the slightest idea what he was going to do; all the same, he raised his feet unusually high and Gregor was astounded by the huge size of his boots' soles. Yet he did not dwell on it, he certainly knew from the first day of his new life, that his father believed he should be treated with the utmost severity; and so he ran before him, faltering when the father stopped and rushing forwards again when he moved slightly. In this way they ran several times around the room, without something decisive ever happening, indeed without the whole thing appearing as a pursuit, since it was so slow. Gregor decided to remain temporarily on the floor, for he particularly feared that his father might mistake a flight over the walls or the ceiling, as a specific form of malice and unpleasantness. Gregor certainly could not endure this race any longer ...for while his father took one step, he had to perform an untold number of movements. A shortness of breath soon became noticeable, as indeed he had never possessed an adequate lung capacity, even in his earlier life. He now lurched about in order to gather strength for the run and he could barely keep his eyes open; in his stupor he did not think of any other way for salvation; he had already almost forgotten that the walls were left free to him; but in this room there were a lot of carefully carved furniture with spikes and knobs. Suddenly something flew past, narrowly missing him and rolling down in front of him. It was an apple; soon after a second one was hurled towards him. Gregor stood still, terrified; running on was useless, for the father had decided to bombard him. He had filled his pockets from the fruit bowl on the sideboard and was throwing apple after apple, without, for the time being, taking an accurate aim. These small red apples fell all over the floor as if electrified, and crashed into each other. An apple, unconvincingly thrown, hit Gregor in the back but slid away harmlessly. Another followed immediately, penetrating Gregor's back; he wanted to drag himself forward to a new place, as if it would be possible to leave this surprising and unbelievable pain behind; however, he felt as if he were pinned down and stretched in complete confusion of all his senses. He only saw with a last glance that the door of his room was torn open, his mother rushing out before his screaming sister, in her undergarments, for the sister had undressed her in order to make her breathe easier after her fainting spell; he then saw how his mother ran to the father, her untied robes falling on the floor one after the other; how she stumbled over them and how she closed in on the father by embracing him - but now Gregor's sight failed him - her hands clasping the back of his head, begging him for mercy and for Gregor's life.

PART 3

Gregor's serious injury, which made him suffer for over a month – the apple remained stuck in his flesh as a visible reminder, given that no-one dared to approach him – seemed to have prompted even the father to realise, that despite his current sad and repulsive condition, Gregor was still a member of the family who should not be treated as a fiend, and that out of familial duty, it was imperative that they swallowed their repugnance and showed patience, nothing but patience.

Though Gregor's injury had probably impaired his mobility for ever, and for the time being it took him much longer to move around his room, just like an invalid – crawling up the walls was out of the question – yet he received, in his opinion, a sufficiently satisfactory compensation from the deterioration in his condition: Every evening, the door to the living room which he used to watch sharply for one or two hours, opened, so that he, lying in the darkness of his room and invisible to those in the living room, could see the whole family at the candle-lit table and listen to their conversation, in a sense by general consent ...well, quite unlike before.

Of course the conversations were not as animated as those in times gone by, the ones Gregor always yearned for in his tiny hotel room, as he threw himself on damp bed clothing. Now they were mostly hushed. The father fell asleep in his armchair soon after dinner; the mother and sister urged each other to be quiet; the mother bent down under the light, sewed fine clothing for a fashion boutique; the sister, who had been employed as a salesgirl, studied stenography and French in the evenings, in order to perhaps find a better job. Sometimes she woke her father up and as he did not realise at all that he had slept, he would tell his wife: 'You have been sewing for such a long time today!' and fall asleep immediately afterwards, while his wife and daughter exchanged a

177

tired smile. With some obstinacy, the father refused to discard his uniform at home; and while the nightgown hung idly on the clothes peg, he dozed off fully dressed, in his seat, as if he were constantly ready for service and waiting even here for his superior's orders. As a result, the not so new uniform, lost its cleanliness despite the mother and sister's diligence and care; and often for long evenings, Gregor gazed at this all blotchy bright uniform with shiny golden buttons, in which the old man slept, most uncomfortably, yet quite serenely.

As soon as the clock struck ten, the mother sought to wake the father with comforting soft words and then persuade him to go to bed, for that was not the proper way to sleep and he, who had to be at work at six o'clock in the morning, really needed a decent night's rest. But in his obstinacy – embraced since becoming a civil servant – he now always insisted on staying longer at the table, despite regularly falling asleep; moreover, it was with the greatest effort that he then exchanged the armchair for the bed. Yet no matter how much the mother and the sister gently admonished him, he shook his head for fifteen minutes, kept his eyes closed and did not stand up. The mother tugged him at the arms, whispered cajoling words in his ear, the sister left her work in order to help her mother but it did not have any effect on the father. He sank ever deeper into his armchair. Not until the women grabbed him by the armpits, did he open his eyes, then, looking alternately at the mother and the sister, he said: 'This is life... this is the tranquillity of my old age'. And propped up by the two women, he stood up laboriously, as if he were the heaviest burden for himself, let himself be led by the women to the door, waved them off and walked on further by himself, while the mother hastily threw down her sewing kit and the sister her pen, in order to run after the father and help him further.

Who on earth had now time to care for Gregor, in this worn out and exhausted family, more than it was absolutely necessary? The household became ever more restricted. The housemaid was laid off; an enormous looking charwoman with white hair fluttering about her head came mornings and evenings in order to do the heaviest work. The mother managed to do everything else, on top of her sewing work. As it happened, various family jewels that the mother and the sister happily wore on festivities, were sold, which Gregor found out one evening, as the family was discussing the prices they had obtained. The main grievance was always the fact they were unable to leave their now all too big house, for it was impossible to relocate Gregor. However, Gregor realised that he was possibly not the only impediment to their relocation, for they could have easily transported him in a suitable crate with a few air holes. What mainly deterred the family from change of residence was instead their complete hopelessness and the notion that they had been afflicted by such a calamity like no one else in their circle of friends and relatives. What the world claimed from hapless people, they fulfilled to the utmost, the father fetched breakfast for the minor bank officials, the mother sacrificed herself by doing the laundry for strangers, the sister ran back and forth, behind the counters, at the bidding of customers... but still the family's efforts were not sufficient. The wound on Gregor's back began hurting afresh, when mother and sister, having taken the father to bed, returned, left their work and sat close to each other, cheek to cheek; when the mother, pointing to Gregor's room, said: 'I beg you Grete, close the door now'; and when Gregor found himself in darkness again, while nearby, the women blended their tears or even stared at the table, dry-eyed.

Gregor's nights and days were almost always sleepless. Sometimes he thought that by the time the door would open the next day, he would again take the entire affairs of the family in hand, just as before; after a long time, the director and the chief clerk, the junior clerks and the apprentice boys, the dim-witted manservant, two or three friends from other trades, a parlour-maid from a provincial hotel, a dear, brief recollection, a cashier in a milliner's shop, whom he had earnestly but much too slowly pursued, all reappeared in his thoughts; they popped out mixed with strangers or forgotten people, but instead of helping him and his family, they were altogether unapproachable... and he was happy when they vanished. Then again he was not in the mood to worry about his family, he was just furious about the unpleasant waiting, and though he did not even know what he craved, he certainly made plans to get into the pantry and grab – even when he was not hungry at all – whatever was due to him. Without at all pondering on what would now please Gregor, every morning and noon, before she rushed to work, the sister hastily pushed some kind of dish into Gregor's room with her foot, and in the afternoon, indifferent to whether the food tasted good or was left totally untouched – which more and more was the case – swept out the leftovers with a swing of the broom. The clean up of the room which she always did in the evenings, could not have been done more hastily. Stretches of dirt ran across the walls and here and there lay bundles of dust and dross. In the early days, upon the entrance of his sister, Gregor would position himself at a particular angle in a sense to reproach her. He could have indeed stayed there for weeks without seeing any improvement in his sister; she of course noticed the dirt as much as he did, but she had now decided to leave it. Yet, with a stroke of sensibility that had awakened in her and which seemed to have stricken the whole family, she reserved for herself the exclusive right of tidying Gregor's room.

Once the mother decided to give Gregor's room a good cleaning – which she did only by using some buckets of water – too much humidity certainly made Gregor ill and he lay embittered and immobile, spread on the sofa, but the punishment for the mother was inevitable; for in the evening, as soon as the sister noticed the change in Gregor's room, highly offended, she ran into the living room and despite the imploring raised hands of the mother, burst into a crying fit; the parents watched her – the father had of course jolted out of his armchair – at first astounded and helpless, until even they started to stir. The father reproached the mother on his right, that she should have relinquished the cleaning of Gregor's room to the sister; on the left he started yelling at the sister that she should never again clean up Gregor's room; meanwhile the mother tried to haul her husband who was beside himself with excitement, into the bedroom; the sister, sobbing uncontrollably, was banging on the table with her little fists; and Gregor started hissing loudly and furiously, that no one had thought about shutting the door and sparing him such a spectacle and disturbance. Even the sister – exhausted by her daily job – wearied about caring for Gregor: There was no need for Gregor's mother to enter his room, or for Gregor to be neglected; for now the charwoman was there. This elderly widow who in her long life had overcome the worst with the help of her strong constitution, actually felt no repulsion for Gregor. Without in any way being curious, she had once accidentally opened the door of his room and at the sight of Gregor – who astounded, began to move back and forth, though no one was chasing him – merely stood back looking, with arms folded.

Since then, she never omitted to briefly open the door, mornings and afternoons, to have a look at Gregor inside. At first she even called out to him, with words which she perhaps perceived as friendly such as 'come here then, you old dung beetle!' or 'look at the good old dung beetle!' To such address, Gregor did not respond at all; he instead stayed still in his place, as if the door had never been opened. He wished this charwoman had been ordered to tidy up his room daily, instead of unnecessarily disturb him every time it took her fancy. One early morning – heavy rain, perhaps a sign of the coming spring, was beating against the window panes – Gregor became so desperate and enraged as the charwoman began with her usual figure of speech, that he, as if to

181

assault her, turned on her, albeit slowly and feebly. The charwoman did not panic however, she just hoisted a chair and the way she stood near the door, with her mouth wide open, her intention was clear: That she would shut her mouth at the same time as she would strike Gregor on the back, with that chair. 'So this will not go any further?' She asked, as Gregor turned around again; she then quietly put the chair down in a corner.

Now Gregor stopped eating almost completely. Only when he accidentally came across some prepared dish, he took a bite as if playing a game, kept it an hour long in his mouth and usually spat it out again. At first he thought it was his sorrow over the state of his room that prevented him from eating, but he soon reconciled with the changes made in his abode. They had become accustomed to bring anything they could not accommodate in other places, to Gregor's room and there were many such things, for they had rented out one room of the house to three lodgers. These earnest men – all three fully bearded, as Gregor had determined through the crack of the door – were meticulous about orderliness, not only in their own room, but since they had now taken lodgings here, they were attentive to the whole state of affairs, particularly in the kitchen. They could not bear at all unnecessary or dirty odds and ends. Furthermore, they had brought over a great deal of their own furnishings. For this reason, many objects that were indeed unsaleable but at the same time could not be thrown away, had become superfluous. All these made their way into Gregor's room: And so arrived the ash pan and the rubbish bin from the kitchen. The charwoman who was always very much in a hurry, simply hurled what appeared useless at first sight, into Gregor's room; fortunately, Gregor usually saw only the objects in question and the hand holding them. Perhaps the charwoman intended to recuperate them if and when they were needed again, or perhaps she wanted to accumulate them so that she could throw them away all at once; but the junk actually remained where it had first been

thrown, unless Gregor moved it around by wriggling through; at
first he was constrained to do so since there was no more space left
free for him to crawl, but later on he did so with great pleasure,
even if such hikes left him exhausted, terribly sad and motionless
for hours afterwards.

Since the lodgers often dined at home, most evenings the door of
the living room remained shut, but Gregor simply did not care
about the door not being open; indeed, he had not taken advantage
of it, even on the occasions when the door had been open; he had
instead, without his family even noticing, laid in the darkest corner
of his room. Once the charwoman had left the door to the living
room slightly open, and it remained so until the lodgers returned in
the evening and switched the light on. They sat down upstairs at
the table, where in times gone by, the father, the mother and
Gregor used to eat; they unfolded the napkins and took the cutlery
in hand. The mother appeared at once with a dish of meat and
close behind her the sister with a dish of layered potatoes. The hot
food was steaming. The lodgers bent over the dishes placed in
front of them as if they wanted to inspect it before eating; in fact
the one in the middle, who seemed to exert some authority over
the two others, cut up a piece of meat, straight from the dish,
clearly to assess whether it was tender enough or should be
returned to the kitchen. He was satisfied, and the mother and the
sister who had anxiously looked on, breathed a sigh of relief and
began laughing.

The family itself ate in the kitchen. Nevertheless, the father came
into the living room, before going in the kitchen, walked about the
table, his cap in hand, with one prolonged curtsy. The lodgers all
stood up and whispered something under their breath. When they
were left alone again, they ate under almost complete silence. It
appeared peculiar to Gregor, that out of all the noises that come
forth in the process of eating, one could mainly discern the sound
of chomping teeth, as if they wanted to prove to Gregor that one

needed teeth for eating and that without teeth, one could achieve nothing, even with the finest toothless jaws. 'I do have an appetite,' Gregor thought sorrowfully to himself... 'but not for these things. How much these lodgers eat, while I perish from starvation!'

On that very afternoon – Gregor did not remember ever having heard the violin during all this time – the sound of the violin playing came from the kitchen. The lodgers had already finished their evening meal, the one in the middle had pulled out a newspaper and given a couple of pages to the other two, and now they were all leaning back and smoking. When the sound of the violin began, they became attentive, got up and went on tiptoe behind the door where they stood still, huddled against each other. They must have been heard from the kitchen, for the father shouted: 'Are the gentlemen bothered by the playing? It could be discontinued at once'. 'On the contrary,' said the middle one, 'why doesn't the young lady come to us and play in the living room where it is for sure more comfortable and cosy?' 'Oh, certainly,' shouted the father, as if he were the violin player. The lodgers returned to the living room and waited. Soon came the father with the music stand, the mother with the music and the sister with the violin. The sister calmly prepared everything for playing; the parents who had never before let rooms and therefore exaggerated in their politeness towards the lodgers, did not at all dare to sit down on their own chairs; the father leaned on the door, the right hand stuck in between two knobs of his buttoned up livery coat; but the mother accepted the chair that one of the gentlemen had offered her and sat where the lodger had actually accidentally placed it, secluded, in a corner.

The sister began to play; father and mother followed attentively the movement of her hands, each from their own side. Gregor, attracted by the music, had dared to advance slightly more and his head was sticking out into the living room. He hardly wondered why he had lately been so inconsiderate towards others; before, being considerate had been a matter of pride to him. Thereby, he would have all the more reason to hide, for as a consequence of the dust that gathered all over his room and flew about with the slightest movement, he too was covered by dust; he pulled strings, hair, food leftovers from his back and sides; his indifference to everything was far greater than earlier on, when he lay on his back several times a day and scrubbed himself on the carpet. Nevertheless, he felt no reserve to move forward onto the spotless flooring of the living room. Despite this, nobody noticed him. The family was fully engaged with playing the violin; the lodgers however, who had initially positioned themselves, hands in pockets, far too close behind his sister's music stand in order to see every single note – which must have surely disturbed her – soon moved back to the window, heads sunken and engaged in quiet conversation; they remained there, under the anxious gaze of the father. It was now blatantly obvious that they had been disappointed in their expectation of hearing a beautiful or entertaining piece of violin music, and they were putting up with this disturbance of their tranquillity, only out of politeness. The way they blew their cigar smoke out of their nose and mouth high in the air, spoke of their nervousness. Yet his sister was playing so beautifully. Her face was inclined to one side and her sad scrutinising eyes were following the stave. Gregor crawled still a bit further and held his head as close to the floor as possible in order to catch a glimpse of her eyes. Was he an animal...to be so smitten by music? This was to him the way to the unknown nourishment he so craved. He was determined to press forward and reach his sister, pull at her skirt and thus indicate to her that she could come into his room with her violin, for no one here appreciated her music as much as he did. He did not want to let her out of his room anymore, at least for as long as he lived; for once his horrible appearance could be useful to him; he wanted to be simultaneously at all the doors and hiss away the aggressors. But his sister should not be forced to stay with him, she should instead be there voluntarily; she should sit by him on the sofa, tilt her ear towards him while he would confide in her that he intended to send her to the music academy and had this misfortune not happened in the meantime, he would have announced it to everyone last Christmas – had Christmas really gone by? – without at all worrying about any opposition. After this explanation Grete would burst into tears and Gregor would raise himself to her shoulder and kiss her neck, which she left bare without any ribbons or collar.

'Mr. Samsa!' shouted the middle lodger, pointing out with his forefinger and without wasting any more words, to Gregor who was slowly moving forward. The violin fell silent, the middle lodger smiled at first, shaking his head and looking at his friends and then he turned his attention to Gregor again. The father thought it would be best to reassure the lodgers for now, instead of shooing Gregor away, for they did not seem agitated at all and found Gregor more entertaining than the violin playing. He rushed towards them seeking to lead them to their room with outstretched arms while at the same time trying to block their view of Gregor with his own body. Now they were actually somewhat angry; it was not clear whether that was due to the father's behaviour or their unexpected discovery that they had had such a neighbour, without ever having suspected it. They demanded clarification from the father, raised their arms, started plucking their beards restlessly and retreated only slowly back to their room. In the meantime, the sister who had been left quite forlorn when her playing was so suddenly interrupted, slowly overcame her shock: She had held the violin and the bow in her slack hanging hands for a while and as if she were still playing, was staring at the music; but at a stroke, she pulled herself together, laid the instrument on the lap of her mother, who due to over-active lungs, was still sitting in the armchair, and ran into the side-room which the lodgers, driven by her father, were fast approaching. Her practised hands were throwing the blankets and the cushions high into the air and the beds were made in no time, before even the lodgers arrived; she then quickly slipped out. The father appeared once again to be so consumed by his obstinacy that he forgot all the rules of respect and accused his lodgers. He shoved them and shoved them right up to the door of their room, until the middle lodger brought him to a stop, stamping his foot thunderously. 'I hereby declare,' he said, raising his hand and seeking the eye of the mother and the sister as well, 'that considering the disgusting conditions in this household... ' – at this point he spat forcefully on the floor – 'I terminate my contract for the room, as of this moment. I will of course not pay a penny for the days that I have lived here, on the contrary, I will still consider bringing claims for damages against you, and believe me, there are reasonable grounds for them'. He then fell silent and looked straight ahead as if he were awaiting something. Actually his two friends immediately chimed in with the words: 'We also give notice to quit, as of this moment'. He then grabbed the door handle and slammed the door shut.

The father fumbled with his hands, staggered back and fell into his armchair. It looked as if he was spreading out for his usual evening nap, but the strong nodding of his unstable head was proof that he was not at all asleep. The whole time Gregor had remained still on the spot where the lodgers had caught him out. His disappointment over his plan's failure, and perhaps also his frailty brought about by starvation, made it impossible for him to move. He already feared with some certainty that at any moment the general tension would unload and collapse on him... and he lay waiting. Not even the ringing sound of the violin, which from under her trembling fingers slid on the mother's lap and fell on the floor, startled him.

'Dear parents,' said the sister, banging her hand on the table by way of an introduction, 'this cannot go on. Perhaps you do not realise, but I do. I will not pronounce my brother's name in front of this beast, and I therefore just say: we should try to get rid of it. We have been patient and done all that was humanly possible to look after it; I do not think anyone could reproach us in the least'.

'She is right, a thousand times,' said the father, for his part. The mother, who as usual had breathing problems, began coughing hollowly into her hand, with an insane look in the eyes. The sister ran to her mother and held her forehead. Having heard his daughter's words, the father seemed decidedly thoughtful; he sat upright, playing with his service cap which lay amongst the plates that were still on the table, since the lodgers' supper... looking from time to time at the motionless Gregor.

'We must try to get rid of it,' said the sister, now exclusively to her father, since her mother, consumed by her coughing fit could not hear anything. 'It will kill both of you, I can see it coming. When we have to work as hard as we all do, we cannot put up with such eternal agony at home. I cannot bear this anymore'; and she burst into such violent sobs that her tears started flowing down the mother's face, whereupon she wiped them off with a natural movement of her hand.

'My child,' said the father compassionately and with remarkable understanding. 'But what should we do?'

In contrast to her former confident self, the sister now shrugged her shoulders as a sign of the helplessness which had overpowered her when she burst into tears.

'If he could understand us,' said the father, half questioningly; still sobbing, the sister waved her hand vigorously as a sign that they should not even think about it.

'If he could understand us,' repeated the father, closing his eyes in order to internalise his daughter's conviction about such an impossibility, 'then perhaps we could come to an agreement with him. But so... '.

'He has to go away,' shouted the sister. 'That is the only way, father. You must try to get rid of the idea that he is Gregor. It is our own misfortune that we believed so... for such a long time; but how can this be Gregor? If it had been Gregor, he would have long ago realised that the cohabitation between human beings and a monster is impossible and he would have gone away of his own accord. We would not have had any brother, but we could have lived on and we would have honoured his memory. Now this creature persecutes us, frightens the lodgers away, apparently wants to take over the house and drive us all onto the street. Look father... ' she suddenly cried out 'he's started moving again!' and in a panic – quite incomprehensible to Gregor – she even left her mother, pushed away the armchair as if preferring to sacrifice her mother rather than staying close to Gregor, and rushed behind her father, who, merely agitated due to her behaviour, also stood up and raised both arms in an attempt to protect his daughter.

Gregor did not have the slightest intention to frighten anyone, let alone his sister. He had merely started to reverse in order to crawl back into his room; this manoeuvre looked somewhat strange since in doing so, he had to repeatedly raise his head and bang it on the floor... and all due to his ailing circumstances. He looked around. His good intentions seemed to have been recognised; it had only been a momentary panic. Now they were all watching him in silence and sorrow. The mother lay in the armchair, her legs outstretched and pressed against each other. She looked jaded and her eyes were almost closing; the father and the sister sat next to each other and she laid her hand on his neck.

'I should perhaps turn around now,' thought Gregor, and began his labour again. He could not suppress the wheezing anymore and now and then had to stop and rest. No one was pressing him, and all was left to him. As he completed the turn, he immediately

189

started to crawl straight on. He was surprised at the long distance which separated him from his room and could not comprehend how he, in his frail condition, had travelled the same stretch, without even noticing it, shortly before.

Constantly mindful of crawling as fast as possible, he barely heeded the fact that not a word, not an outcry by his family had perturbed him. As soon as he was past his door, he turned his head around, not completely, since he felt his neck stiffen, but enough to see all the same, that behind him nothing had changed, only his sister had stood up. His last glance caught the sight of his mother who by now was fast asleep.

Hardly was he inside his room that the door was hastily shut and locked. Gregor was so frightened by the sudden noise behind him that his little legs began folding. It was his sister who had hurried over. She had stood there upright and had waited... she had then light-footedly leapt forward – Gregor had not heard her coming at all – and shouted out to her parents 'Finally!' as she turned the key in the lock.

'And what now?' Gregor asked himself, looking around him in the dark. He discovered at once that he could not budge at all. He was not surprised by it, since it had always seemed unnatural to him that he could actually move along with such thin little legs. Besides, he felt relatively comfortable. He had of course aches and pains in his whole body, but it appeared that they were gradually diminishing and finally even disappearing. He could not feel anymore the rotten apple stuck into his back and the ensuing infected sore which was now completely covered by soft dust. He reminisced about his family with love and warmth. He was now even more resolute than his sister in the belief that he should disappear. He remained in this state of placid and vacant reflection until the tower clock struck three in the morning. He experienced the breaking of dawn from his window. Then his head sank involuntarily down... and his last breath streamed feebly out of his nostrils.

When the charwoman arrived early the following morning – she banged the doors shut with such strength and haste, though she had often been requested to avoid it, that it became impossible for anyone to have a peaceful sleep – she did not at first notice anything exceptional when she as usual visited Gregor for a short time. She assumed he was laying motionless on purpose, pretending to sulk. She credited him with wits and great intelligence. As she happened to hold a broom in her hand, she tried to tickle him away from the door. When she did not see any reaction, she became angry and poked into him even harder and she only became alert when she had pushed him out of his usual space, without him putting up any resistance. As soon as she realised the true circumstances, she opened her eyes wide, whistled away to herself, but did not stay on too long, instead she tore the bedroom door open, screaming with her powerful voice, in the dark: 'Look at him, he is dead, he is outright dead!'

Mr. and Mrs. Samsa sat upright on the marital bed; they had to get around the horror of what the charwoman had just announced, before being able to take it in. But they then got hastily out of bed, each from either side, Mr. Samsa throwing the blanket over his shoulders, Mrs. Samsa coming out from behind in her nightgown, and so they entered Gregor's room. Meanwhile the door to the living room, where Grete had been sleeping since the lodgers' arrival, also opened. She was fully dressed as if she had not slept at all, as it was also evident from her pallid face. 'Dead?' said Mrs. Samsa, looking quizzically at the charwoman, though she could inspect and acknowledge everything herself, even without proof. 'I reckon he is,' said the charwoman, and as proof, she pushed Gregor's corpse to one side with her broom. Mrs. Samsa made a sudden move as if wanting to halt the broom, but did not do it. 'Now,' said Mr. Samsa, 'now we can pay our thanks to God'. He crossed himself and the three women followed his example. Grete who had not stopped staring at the corpse, said: 'Just look how skinny he is. Well, it is such a long time since he has eaten anything; the food came in and went out just the same'. Effectively, Gregor's corpse was dry and completely flat, and one noticed only now that he was not high on his little legs anymore, and nothing else distracted an acute glance.

'Grete come join us for a minute,' said Mrs. Samsa with a wistful smile; and Grete followed her parents into the bedroom, without stopping to look back and stare at the corpse. The charwoman shut the door and opened the window wide. Though it was early in the morning, the fresh air had a certain softness about it. It was now already the end of March.

The three lodgers walked out of their room and looked around surprised, in anticipation of breakfast; they had been forgotten. 'Where is our breakfast?' the middle lodger asked the charwoman glumly. The latter lay her finger on her mouth, then hastily but silently beckoned them over to Gregor's room. They entered the room which was by now quite bright, and stood around Gregor's corpse, their hands in the pockets of their threadbare little jackets. Then the bedroom door opened and Mr. Samsa appeared in his livery, his wife on the one arm and his daughter on the other. They were all slightly tear stained; Grete pressed her face from time to time on the father's arm.

'Leave my house immediately,' shouted Mr. Samsa showing them the door, without letting the women off his arms. 'What do you mean?' said the middle lodger somewhat bewildered, smiling cloyingly. The other two kept their hands behind them, rubbing them uninterruptedly together, as if in joyful anticipation of a serious row which would end up in their favour. 'I mean exactly what I said,' replied Mr. Samsa, going in a straight line towards the lodger, accompanied by his companions. The lodger stood still at first, staring at the floor, as if he were reordering his thoughts in his head. 'Then we are off,' he said and looked up at Mr. Samsa, perhaps demanding his approval for such a decision, in a sudden rush of humility. Mr. Samsa merely nodded several times in quick succession, looking at him wide-eyed. Thereupon the lodger walked at once into the hallway, with long strides; his two friends, their hands now quite still, had been listening in and they scuttled after him, fearful that Mr. Samsa could walk in and disturb their unity with their leader. In the hallway, the three of them removed their hats from the clothes rack, pulled their walking sticks from the umbrella stand, took a bow in silence and left the house. With an – as it happened – quite unfounded mistrust, Mr. Samsa and the two women came out onto the landing; leaning on the railing, they watched how the three gentlemen slowly but surely descended along the staircase, disappeared at a certain bend of each floor and appeared again within a few seconds; the deeper they descended, the more indifferent to them the Samsas became, and as an apprentice butcher, holding his fare proudly on his head came upstairs, Mr. Samsa and the women swiftly left the handrail and they all returned to the home, quite relieved.

They decided to spend the day resting and going for a stroll; they did not only deserve this interruption of work, they in fact really needed it. So they sat at the table and wrote three sick notes: Mr. Samsa to his board of management, Mrs. Samsa to her employer, and Grete to her boss. While they were writing, the charwoman came in to say that she was going to depart since her morning job had come to an end. The three writers at first merely nodded, without looking up; only when they saw that the charwoman was waffling, did they eye her, angrily. 'What now?' asked Mr. Samsa. The charwoman stood at the door, smiling, as if she could announce an important happy message to the family but would only do so, if requested. The almost upright ostrich feather on her hat, which used to so irritate Mr. Samsa even during her term of service, was swaying in all directions. 'So what do you really want now?' asked Mrs. Samsa, whom the charwoman respected most. 'Yes,' answered the charwoman who could not talk further in her fit of friendly laughter.

'Well, you should not worry about how to throw away that stuff next door. Everything has been taken care of'. Mrs. Samsa and Grete bowed down on their letters as if they wanted to continue writing; Mr. Samsa who had noticed that the charwoman now intended to describe everything in detail, warded her off firmly with outstretched hands. Since she was not allowed to elaborate, she suddenly remembered that she was in a great hurry and cried out, obviously offended: 'Adieu, everybody'; she turned around wildly and left the house, banging the door with a frightening sound.

'She will be dismissed tonight,' said Mr. Samsa, but he did not receive any reply neither from his wife nor his daughter, for it seemed that the charwoman had again disturbed their newly acquired tranquillity. They got up, went to the window and stayed there embracing each other. Mr. Samsa turned around in his armchair towards them and observed them for some time. Then he called out: 'Come here then. Leave the old things and for God's sake give a bit of attention to me'. The women quickly complied, rushed towards him, caressed him and swiftly finished their letters.

Then the three of them left the house together – something they had not done in months – and went to the countryside by tram. The warm sun was bathing the tramcar in which they were the only passengers. They discussed, comfortably leaning back on their seats, the prospects for the future and it seemed that on close reflection, these were not bad at all, for their jobs which they had actually never discussed together before, were extremely reasonable and quite promising for the future. The greatest immediate improvement in their position would of course be attained through moving house; now they needed a smaller, cheaper, but better located and more practical house than this one, which had been Gregor's choice. While they were chatting, it occurred to Mr. and Mrs. Samsa, quite simultaneously, that their lively daughter, despite all their recent troubles, had blossomed into a beautiful and voluptuous young lady. They became quieter and unconsciously, by exchanging knowing glances, thought that it was now time to find a good honest husband for her. At the destination of their ride, just like a confirmation of their new dreams and good intentions, it was first their daughter who rose up and stretched her young body.

INTERPRETATION

Metamorphosis is indeed a story of transformation, but one that illustrates more than the mere superficial alteration of the main character's appearance. The story reveals how an unexpected turn of events leads to a young man undergoing a complete physical change, resulting in an inner transformation that brings immediately contentment, and a total change of tastes; for now he no longer possesses the needs and wants of his old self, but instead embraces his new life completely. His family undergo their own metamorphosis as a consequence of Gregor's change, for they are forced to come to terms with circumstances not of their making, nor with a foreseeable solution; as the initial shock and bewilderment settle, they are compelled to strive for their own independence, no longer being able to rely on the comfortable support of their hard-working son and brother. Kafka does not concern himself with the events leading up to Gregor's metamorphosis, nor with the reason why this change has taken place, but instead focuses on the aftermath of this person's significant transformation. Is it conceivable that Kafka used *Metamorphosis* to illustrate a significant and sudden change within himself at some point in his life? A transformation so powerful on the inside, so deep and impacting on his life, that it not only transformed him, but also those closest to him; for now he took on a completely different appearance, seeming unrecognisable; yet he felt completely at ease with this change, feeling an immediate contentment.

Gregor's transformation brought him freedom; as he was unable to continue functioning as he did in human form, the obligations and responsibilities that he carried on his human shoulders now rolled off his smooth rounded armour-like back; much to the dismay of his family who depended so heavily on their sole beneficiary, but now find themselves in difficult circumstances. Could this reflect Kafka's own experience, his transformation compelling him to pursue a different path, drawing him away from his old obligations, causing those closest to him to change as well when their dependence on him slipped away? A reference to Kafka's duty to uphold his obligations to his family may be when Gregor is unable to present himself for work, worrying the family so much that they feel forced to call to him: What initially appears to be innocent concern from his curious and bewildered family, soon turns into a barrage of frantic enquiry; their voices demanded an answer, reminding him of his duties, growing evermore angry and impatient, unrelenting in their quest for his acknowledgement. The man within the metamorphosis was indeed trapped, in a body beyond comprehension, in the midst of a family beyond reason, and ultimately, in a quandary with no tenable solution. Did Kafka feel the pressure from so many sides of his family, as he no longer conformed to the convention of their expectations? For when he was locked away in the depths of his transformation, others still bombarded him from many sides and demanded his attention.

Kafka takes great care to detail how Gregor adapted to his already familiar, but now, newly traversed surroundings after his transformation, depicting him as a more contented soul after the change. Is Kafka revealing his own comfort after his change, as he moves through familiar terrain in what he considers to be his new, vastly transformed self? Gregor tried to reach out to his family, desperately wishing to spare them from the grief and pain they felt, choosing to hide away so as to minimise their heartache; he needed to reassure them that he meant them no harm, only wishing for their understanding; though he deserved their compassion, he was only ever considered as no more than an insect. Does Kafka reveal how he feels those closest ... treated him? Perhaps he felt he was considered as nothing more than an insignificant insect by others, and so chose Gregor to be transformed into one; or maybe it was Kafka's own self-loathing that cast him as his own victim under these circumstances.

The unique mechanism of Kafka's mind is one that most can only ever imagine... but never truly understand; such a mind refuses to be confined within the walls of mediocrity, but is instead governed by a tempestuous restlessness that demands freedom to express itself. Kafka may have referred to this when Gregor's appetite changes – after his metamorphosis – and he initially only finds food that is sour or rotten palatable, eventually losing his appetite altogether. The change in taste for Gregor may represent the food for thought in Kafka's mind, where the conventional thought of the day that was once so tolerable, now becomes unpalatable, subsequently causing a complete loss of appetite: The mediocrity of conventional attitudes and opinions, coupled with the bland conversation he encounters... could no longer be served to Kafka, as the sustenance he now requires to be nourished with... is for a different intellectual beast. Where Gregor notes how the lodgers eat so well while he is left hungry, may imply Kafka recognised how others feasted so heartily on the mundane conversation of the day, while his intellectual hunger was now rarely satisfied.

Gregor's family are forced to undergo their own metamorphosis as a result of his transformation: Their reaction to this disturbing situation turns from shock and despair to frustration and resentment; their initial concerns for the welfare of their son and brother soon turn into selfish interest for their own preservation, as they eventually abandon him, for he has become an unbearable burden. It is important to note that despite his family's reaction, Gregor felt very comfortable for his metamorphosis: Even from the beginning, he sought to adapt as quickly as possible to his new circumstances, feeling no distress for what had happened to him; he now felt liberty in his new form... instead of the imprisonment he endured in his old one. The tremendous responsibility placed on Gregor – to provide for his family financially as well as meet the obligations of his parents' debt to his employer – ensured he was no longer an individual with the potential to live freely... but a duty bound servant to others. How shocking that shame and fear blinded the family's judgement so much that they chose to shut him away instead of rallying to his aid! Regardless of whether the young man was within the realms of help is irrelevant; surely his welfare should have been considered above the reputation of the family. The family show their resourcefulness in their time of need by taking jobs to provide for themselves; they clearly could have contributed to their financial circumstances all along, but chose to place the responsibility on Gregor while they waited for him to resolve their debts and provide for them. They took in lodgers to assist with their financial commitments, though ironically, by doing this they substituted their dependence on Gregor for the dependence on others; unless they strive for complete self-reliance they would be destined to remain at the mercy of others to provide for them. Only when the lodgers where asked to leave, forcing the family to rely solely on their own income and move to a more affordable home, could they finally appreciate their freedom through self-sufficiency.

The most disturbing aspect of this story is revealed at the end, where the family show not only such little grief for Gregor's demise, but instead relief at his passing: How could their feelings for their son have degenerated so significantly? Gregor's demise is not only tragic... but also bizarre, as he wasted away to nothing more than an empty shell. Could this be a telling reference by Kafka to the tuberculosis that ravaged his body, draining him of his very essence... allowing him to waste away to nothing? Or did this situation refer to Kafka recognising that his relationship with those he had once so much in common, wasted away to an empty shell, as they no longer shared intellectual compatibility!

Metamorphosis: A story of change, the tale of transformation, not only illustrating the plight of these characters... but the lives of many. This peculiar and somewhat disturbing story powerfully stirs the imagination, intriguing the reader to contemplate how one would cope under the same circumstances: Waking to find oneself transformed into an insect, completely unable to function as before, unable to communicate with those closest and dearest, instead scaring and bewildering them, or, to be confronted by a creature, only to find it is a cherished relative struck down by an unforeseen misfortune for which one can do nothing to help. We could certainly empathise with either party, but hope never to find ourselves in either's place! Change is an inevitable part of life; as one matures... one evolves, physically, emotionally and intellectually. This transformation can be gradual and gentle... or sudden and dramatic, but either can incite an uncomfortable reaction in those closest to us, causing them to change; for they may feel forced to adjust to a different version of the person they were once used to, as we no longer share common ground. *Metamorphosis* not only enlightens the experience of change, but also encourages understanding of how we change: Change is natural to our existence; to appreciate this process – whether in ourselves or in others – fosters compassion and unity, and precludes condemning those who are no longer considered conventional, and thought of as grotesque... into desolate isolation.

METAMORPHOSIS

My transformation, so unforeseen
Altering my body, but not my whole being

Changing my life, not my love... nor emotion
Still a dutiful son ...filled with loyal devotion

I once had ambitions and hopes, to be realised
Now serving no purpose, I am ostracised

Turned into a prisoner, locked away like a beast
A burden to others, they consider me least

Losing my faith, my direction and drive
No more use to this world... ought I stay alive?

I reach out for love, for any warmth they may share
But no hand comes to meet me... for they do not care!

Existing in silence... with scarcely a mention
No soul to my rescue ...nor humane intervention

As I lay here in darkness, slowly wasting away
Counting the hours, and each day... by day

An appetite lost, for humanities' tastes
Sustained by the spoils... of their leftover wastes

The shell of my being, is now all that is left
The remains of a life...that is now long bereft

And now my life is over, they are free and long gone
They rejoice in my passing, but I did them no wrong!

My Metamorphosis... had left me estranged
For my family's feelings, had wholeheartedly changed

My service to them, as a brother and son
Is now all but forgotten, for now I am done!